PADDINGTON™ 2

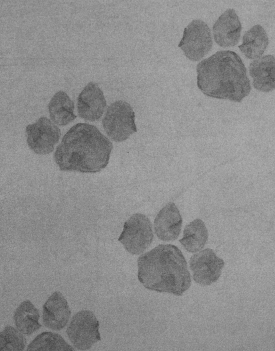

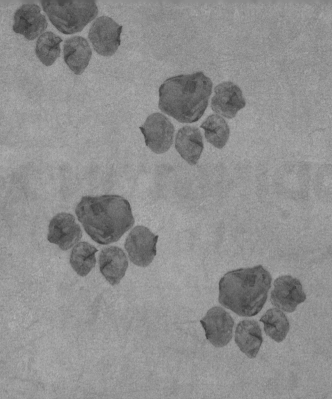

HarperFestival is an imprint of HarperCollins Publishers.

Paddington 2: The Junior Novel
Based on Paddington Bear created by Michael Bond
© Paddington and Company Limited/Studiocanal S.A.S. 2017
Paddington Bear™, Paddington™ and PB™ are trademarks of
Paddington and Company Limited
Licensed on behalf of Studiocanal S.A.S. by Copyrights Group

ISBN: 978-0-06-282433-2

17 18 19 20 21 BVG 10 9 8 7 6 5 4 3
❖
First Edition

PADDiNGTON™ 2
THE JUNIOR NOVEL

Adapted by Anna Wilson
Based on the screenplay written by
Paul King and Simon Farnaby
Based on Paddington Bear
created by Michael Bond

HARPER FESTIVAL
An Imprint of HarperCollinsPublishers

TABLE OF

CONTENTS

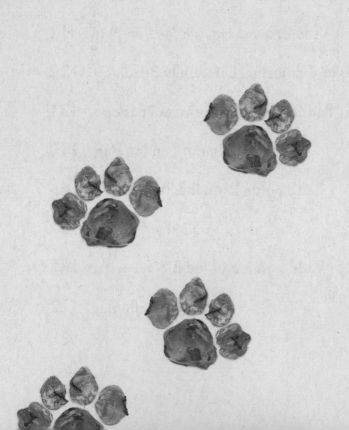

PROLOGUE

A long time ago and a long way away in the Amazon jungle, two elderly bears were sitting on a rope bridge enjoying their tea. They were looking out over the spectacular valley beneath them, where the fast-flowing Amazon River had burst its banks. Water cascaded from all sides, filling the land with roaring floodwaters that rushed toward a magnificent waterfall.

"Our last rainy season," said Pastuzo with a sigh. He took a sip of his tea as he gazed at the landscape.

Lucy nodded and handed her husband a marmalade sandwich. "Just think, Pastuzo. This time next month, we'll be in London!"

"Where the rivers run with marmalade and the streets are paved with bread," he replied.

Lucy shot him a quizzical look. "Did you *read* that book about London?" she asked.

Pastuzo shrugged. "I skimmed it," he said carelessly.

Lucy shook her head. "Oh, Pastuzo!" she scolded him gently.

"Well, reading makes me sleepy," Pastuzo replied awkwardly. "But any city that comes up with this"—he held up the remains of his marmalade sandwich—"is all right with me."

Lucy opened her mouth to reply, but stopped. She gasped and pointed at something she had spotted in the river below. "Oh look, Pastuzo!"

Pastuzo grabbed a pair of binoculars from beside him and peered through them. He couldn't believe what he was seeing. "It's a . . . it's a cub!" he said.

Sure enough, far below the rope bridge there was a tiny baby bear struggling to stay afloat in the rushing river. He was clinging desperately to a bit of driftwood. And the river was pulling him closer and closer to some rocks . . .

Pastuzo lowered his binoculars. He turned to speak to his wife only to see she had left her place on the bridge and was already climbing down a trailing vine toward the waters beneath!

"Lucy!" Pastuzo shouted.

"Lower me down," said Lucy firmly.

Pastuzo could see there was no point in arguing with her. "All right. But be careful!" he cried.

His heart in his mouth, he untied the vine and began

lowering Lucy toward the torrent that raged below. The cub was struggling harder than ever to stay on the branch, but he lost his grip and slipped into the water. Lucy was still a few yards above him as the little cub managed to reach out and grasp the branch again.

"Lower, Pastuzo! Lower!" Lucy called up to her brother.

The cub raised his eyes to see Lucy coming toward him on the vine, reaching out her paw to him. He stretched out to take hold of her, but slipped and sank beneath the water.

Lucy grabbed the little cub as he surfaced and swiftly pulled him from the swirling waters. But above her Pastuzo lost his balance on the bridge. His hat flew off as he toppled . . . He closed his eyes and flailed around with his paws, grabbing on to the bridge and catching hold of it just in time to stop himself from falling.

He opened one eye, hardly daring to look at the scene unfolding below. To his huge relief he saw Lucy still clinging on to the vine. She had his hat, and something else too.

"Lucy? Lucy!" Pastuzo cried.

Lucy smiled up at him. "I'm afraid we're not going to London after all," she said.

Pastuzo frowned. "Why not?"

Lucy looked down at the soaking wet little bundle in her arms. Her eyes filled with love as she took in the tiny face of the bear cub, partly covered by Pastuzo's hat. "We've got a cub to raise," she said.

Pastuzo peered at the little bear. "What's he like?"

"Rather small . . . ," said Lucy. The cub sneezed, and the hat fell over his face. "And rather sneezy!" said Lucy with a laugh.

She lifted the hat to see that the cub had found one of Pastuzo's emergency marmalade sandwiches and was tucking in with relish.

"He likes his marmalade," said Lucy.

"That's a good sign," said Pastuzo, smiling.

"Oh yes, Pastuzo," said Lucy. "If we look after this bear, I have a feeling he'll go far."

CHAPTER 1

At Home with the Browns

Paddington was sitting in his attic room in 32 Windsor Gardens, where he lived with the Brown family, thinking about his old life back in Darkest Peru. He looked out over the city of London— he really did have the most spectacular view from his window.

"How you would love this place, Aunt Lucy," Paddington said aloud. "I do wish you could leave the Home for Retired Bears and visit me here." He knew this was not possible, though. He sighed. "I'll just have to write to you and tell you all my news instead," he said.

And with that, Paddington grabbed some paper and a pen and began a letter to his aunt.

Dear Aunt Lucy,

I am settling in nicely with the Browns, although I still miss you dreadfully. Mrs. Bird's marmalade is excellent, but it will never be quite the same as yours.

It has been a very busy summer. Mrs. Brown has been swimming in the Serpentine lake in Hyde Park. She is training to swim all the way to France. Personally, I don't see the point, as there is a perfectly adequate ferry service, but she insists that is not the same. She's just finished illustrating an adventure story, so maybe that has inspired her.

Judy was going to start a newspaper with her boyfriend, Tony, this summer, but he "dumped" her, apparently—although she says she "dumped" him. She spends a lot of time crying and at one point she said she was going to become a nun! Thankfully she seems to have changed her mind about that and she is going to start the newspaper on her own.

Jonathan is joining Judy at big school this autumn. He has spent the summer building an amazing model railway, but no one is allowed to talk about it as it's "not cool." He says that if anyone asks, he is now called "J-Dog," likes "kung fu and aliens" and is "definitely not into steam trains." I have decided to stop asking him anything for now, in case I get it wrong.

Mr. Brown has been very busy too. There have been big changes at the insurance company where he works. Mr. Brown was very much hoping to get a promotion to become the head of Risk Analysis but a much younger man called Steve Visby got it instead. Ever since, Mr. Brown's behavior has also been quite strange. He now blends his food, paints his hair a funny color, and wears Lycra clothing to go to an exercise class called Chakrabatics. He says it is "all a question of opening your mind and your legs will follow," although his legs looked a bit reluctant to follow him anywhere after the things he had asked them to do.

In spite of all these peculiar goings-on, London really is everything you hoped for and more, Aunt Lucy. Everyone is so kind to me—I have made a lot of very good friends here in Windsor Gardens. I only wish I could introduce you to them all.

I hope that you are well and enjoying life in the Home for Retired Bears. I must sign off now, as I'm on a Very Important Mission. I am afraid it is Top Secret, so I can't tell you about it—yet!

Lots of love,

Padingtun

CHAPTER 2

Paddington's Morning Routine

Everything Paddington had told his Aunt Lucy was true: he was very much at home now at 32 Windsor Gardens. The Browns were a lovely family, and their house was wonderfully warm and welcoming. Paddington especially loved his bedroom in the attic. He enjoyed nothing more than to sit and look out of the little round window across the city he had grown to love.

"Ah, London!" he sighed, gazing out one morning in early autumn. "Another lovely day ahead," he said as he hopped down from the window and took himself to the bathroom to get ready.

He brushed his teeth and gargled with mouthwash, as he did every morning. He smiled to himself as he remembered the first time he had been let loose in the Browns' bathroom. On that occasion, he had swallowed a whole bottle of mouthwash and had managed to flood the bathroom too! He wasn't going to make *those* sorts of mistakes again. Oh, no. He knew how to behave these days, he thought, picking up Mrs. Bird's DustBuster and cleaning his armpits.

His morning routine completed, Paddington ran out to the landing and leaped onto the banister. He slid all the way down to the ground floor, where a delicious breakfast of freshly made marmalade sandwiches was waiting for him.

"Thank you, Mrs. Bird!" he cried, raising his hat. "You certainly know how to make a breakfast fit for a bear."

"You're welcome, dearie," said Mrs. Bird, beaming.

She brushed at some crumbs on her apron and watched fondly as Paddington tucked in with gusto.

Judy and Jonathan, the Browns' children, came in and sat with Paddington. They were dressed ready for the first day of a new school year. Judy looked excited and happy for the first time in a long while.

"Guess what, Paddington?" she said. "The steam fair's coming to town! I'm going to go along tonight and write about it for my newspaper."

"Who's going to want to read about *that*?" Jonathan muttered.

Judy curled her lip at her brother. "Everyone!" she said. "They travel the world in an old steam train. I thought *you'd* love it," she added.

"I do, but don't tell anyone, okay? Not cool," said

Jonathan.

Judy opened her mouth to comment but her mother came into the room just in time to prevent a row.

"Why don't we all go?" asked Mrs. Brown cheerily.

"Good idea," said Mr. Brown, coming in behind his wife and grabbing a piece of toast.

Mrs. Brown smiled lovingly at her husband. "Your father's a dab hand at the coconut shy," she said to her children. "'Bull's-eye Brown' they used to call him."

Judy rolled her eyes.

"Ooh, not anymore," said Henry, shaking his head. "Coconuts are a young man's game." He mimed throwing a ball and immediately winced as he felt a twinge in his shoulder.

Paddington was watching him with interest. "Well, I think you're in great shape for a man your age, Mr. Brown," he said.

"Thank you, Paddington," said Mr. Brown with feeling. Then he did a double take. "Hang on," he said, narrowing his eyes. "How old do you think I am?"

Paddington wasn't sure about being put on the spot like this. Bears were not very good at guessing people's ages. "Oh . . . about eighty?"

"Eighty?" Mr. Brown spluttered.

"At least!" said Paddington with growing confidence.

He pushed back his chair and made to leave the table, putting a marmalade sandwich under his hat for emergencies.

Mrs. Bird turned round from the stove. "Just a minute, wee bear. I thought I told you to clean behind your ears?" she asked, pretending to be stern.

Paddington frowned. "But I did, Mrs. Bird. I—"

Mrs. Bird leaned over and reached behind Paddington's right ear. "I don't know . . . ," she said. "I think you missed a bit. What's that I can see?" And she pulled back, revealing a shiny fifty-pence piece.

Paddington's eyes widened. "My goodness me. I wonder how that got in there?"

Mrs. Bird handed him the coin. "Best keep it somewhere safe, dearie," she said with a smile.

"I will," said Paddington, slipping it into his dufflecoat pocket. "Have a good day, everyone! I must dash, as I am on a Very Important Mission today."

As the family waved him off, Mr. Brown could still be heard muttering, "Eighty . . . I ask you!"

Paddington's mornings had developed a nice rhythm. He knew everyone in the neighborhood these days, and could almost set his watch by who he would see on his way to Mr. Gruber's antique shop.

He stood on the corner of the road, looking out for

Mademoiselle Dupont, who always cycled by at eight-thirty sharp. Seeing her coming, Paddington called out, *"Bonjour, mademoiselle!"*

"Bonjour, Paddington!" said the glamorous lady. She slowed down just enough for him to be able to jump onto the back of her bike, as he did every morning.

As they sped along, Paddington kept an eye out for Dr. Jafri. The doctor was an absentminded man who left his house at the same time every day—and always forgot his keys. Luckily for him, Paddington was always there to remind him.

Today was no different from any other day. Dr. Jafri was walking out of his front door as Paddington passed by. The door was just about to close on the doctor, locking him out, when Paddington called, "Your keys, Dr. Jafri!"

"Keys?" The doctor frowned and patted his pockets, then realized he'd done it again. "Keys!" he shouted, turning back to catch his door just before it slammed shut. "What would I do without you, Paddington?" he said with a shake of his head.

"You're welcome!" said Paddington, raising his hat as he and Mademoiselle Dupont went on their way.

Next he spotted the Peters sisters—two bubbly Jamaican women who watered their orange plants every morning without fail. And there they were, watering and pruning and sniffing tentatively at the ripening fruit.

"Good morning, Miss Peters! Miss Peters!" Paddington cried.

One Miss Peters picked an orange and threw it at Paddington. "Ripe yet?" she asked.

Paddington gave the fruit an appreciative sniff. "Not yet—Tuesday," he said, bowling the orange back.

The sisters thanked him and waved him on his way.

It was here that Paddington always said goodbye to Mademoiselle Dupont, because their routes diverged. She went on to Knightsbridge whereas Paddington was heading to Mr. Gruber's shop on the Portobello Road.

"Thank you, *mademoiselle*!" he said, raising his hat as he jumped from the back of her bike.

"You're welcome, *monsieur*," she said. *"Au revoir!"*

Paddington walked past the Colonel, who was on his way back from the newspaper kiosk where he went every day to buy his morning paper. Paddington, ever cheery, shouted, "Glorious day, Colonel!"

The Colonel was a gloomy disheveled man with a large mustache. He rarely had much to say for himself and today was no different. "Glorious?" he repeated. "Is it, Bear? How absolutely thrilling."

Paddington raised his hat and walked on to the kiosk himself to pick up a copy of the *Daily News*.

He greeted the owner. "Hello, Miss Kitts! Such a lovely day. Do you have any plans?"

Before Miss Kitts could reply a colorful parrot stuck its head out from behind her shoulder and squawked. "Looking for love! Looking for love!"

"Oi, Feathers! You cheeky bird!" Miss Kitts laughed and flapped one hand at the noisy bird. "He's a nightmare, that parrot. Ignore him!" she said to Paddington. "Here you are, love," she added, handing Paddington his paper. "What about you—got any plans?"

"I have, as it happens," said Paddington. "I am on a Very Important Mission."

"Sounds exciting!" said Miss Kitts.

Just then, Paddington's friend, Fred Barnes the garbage collector, pulled up in his garbage truck.

"What's that about a mission?" he asked.

"I am on one. And it involves Mr. Gruber," Paddington said cryptically.

"Intriguing!" said Fred. "Why don't you hop into the lorry? I'll give you a lift. I need to practice all the short-cuts for my test."

"What test?" Paddington asked.

"I'm going to be a London cabbie! Here—" Fred passed Paddington an A–Z map of London. "You can test me on the knowledge while I drive."

CHAPTER 3

A Surprise Find at Mr. Gruber's Shop

Paddington thanked Fred as he hopped down from the garbage truck. He had arrived at Mr. Gruber's antique shop just in time for elevenses, which was the best time of day to visit.

"Ah, Mr. Brown, come in!" said Mr. Gruber, looking up as Paddington walked through the door. "You'll join me for a cup of cocoa and an iced bun?"

"Yes, please, Mr. Gruber," said Paddington.

"So, what can I do for you today?" the shopkeeper asked. He poured steaming cocoa into two mugs and handed Paddington a plate of buns.

"I am on a Very Important Mission," Paddington said. He took a bun and bit into it. "It is my Aunt Lucy's one hundredth birthday soon and I want to find her the perfect present," he explained, his voice muffled with crumbs. "I thought you would be the person to ask for some help."

"Well, you've come to the right place," said Mr. Gruber, beaming. He took a sip of his drink. "See all these boxes?" He gestured to the pile of crates and packages on the floor. "They belong to Madame Kozlova. She runs the fair that has just come to town—have you seen it?"

"Not yet, Mr. Gruber," said Paddington, wiping his whiskers. "Mr. Brown did mention something about it, now I come to think of it. Perhaps we'll be going soon."

"You should. It's magnificent," said the old shop-keeper. "Anyway, come and look at this." He beckoned Paddington over to the boxes. "Madame was having a clear-out and she found these old crates of memory-bilia. There might be something in here that would be just right for Aunt Lucy's special birthday."

Paddington growled in interest. "What a lovely idea!" he said. He took off his hat and put it on the table. He had spotted an old Van de Graaff generator that rather took his fancy, but when he went to touch it, it made his fur stand on end. He quickly withdrew his paw.

"Oh, look at this!" Mr. Gruber was holding up a mechanical monkey on a trapeze.

Paddington put his head on one side. "It's very nice, but—"

Mr. Gruber replaced the monkey and smiled. "I know, it has to be perfect."

Paddington nodded. "Since Uncle Pastuzo died I'm the only relative Aunt Lucy's got left. And it's not every day a bear turns a hundred."

"Quite so," Mr. Gruber agreed.

Paddington rummaged in another trunk and found a wig and some glasses. He took off his hat and put them on, modeling them for his friend.

Mr. Gruber laughed. "And how about some rolling shoes to go with the outfit?" He handed Paddington some roller skates.

Paddington peered over the top of the glasses and said, "Please, Mr. Gruber. Be serious."

Mr. Gruber bit his cheeks and forced himself to stop grinning at his funny friend. "Yes, perhaps her rolling days are behind her," he said with a nod.

Paddington carried on sifting through the contents of one of the packing cases. "Oh, what's this?" he asked, fishing out an old book. "It's beautiful! Look at the picture on the cover. It's a book about London—oh!" he cried again as he opened the pages and the pictures jumped out at him.

Mr. Gruber laughed. "It's a popping book, Mr. Brown," he said.

"It certainly is," said Paddington. He opened and closed the book, marveling at the way the pictures popped up into intricate three-dimensional scenes.

Mr. Gruber came and stood over his shoulder. "That

must be the special popping book Madame Kozlova has told me about. Her great-grandmother was an artist, you see. Every time she visited a city she made a popping book. This must be the one she made of London."

Paddington's eyes lit up as he opened page after page, all of them popping up to reveal different famous London landmarks. "There's Tower Bridge . . . and St. Paul's Cathedral . . . and Buckingham Palace . . . This is wonderful, Mr. Gruber! Aunt Lucy always wanted to visit London but she never had the chance. If she had this book, it would be as though she was really here."

Paddington peered closely at the detail in the pop-ups. He imagined himself shrinking to the size of one of the tiny people in the illustrations. Then he pictured himself with Aunt Lucy. He would take her on the underground and to Piccadilly Circus and the Houses of Parliament. She would clap her paws together in delight and cry, "Oh, it's just as I always dreamed! Thank you, dear nephew."

Mr. Gruber cleared his throat, bringing Paddington back to reality with a jolt. Paddington's eyes were glistening with emotion. He pointed to a line on the book jacket that read "Where All Your Dreams Come True."

"This is the perfect present, Mr. Gruber. Aunt Lucy's going to love it," he said.

"Ah," said Mr. Gruber, consulting the price list. His

face fell. "Ah. This is the only one of its kind. I'm sorry to say they want rather a lot of money for it."

Paddington fished out the coin Mrs. Bird had found that morning. "Would this be enough? Mrs. Bird pulled it from my ear. Perhaps there's more where it came from?" He rummaged enthusiastically in his ear to check, but had no luck.

Mr. Gruber sighed and shook his head. "I'm afraid you're going to need rather more than one earful—a thousand earfuls would be nearer the mark."

"But that's two thousand iced buns!" exclaimed Paddington.

"Let's take another look at the monkey," said Mr. Gruber kindly. "I think he's super-duper." He turned the handle and it came off in his hand. "I can fix that," he said hastily.

Paddington smiled sadly. "That's very kind of you, Mr. Gruber, but Aunt Lucy did a lot for me when I was younger. I want her to know I have made a special effort for her hundredth birthday." He put his hat back on and made for the door. Then, turning back to his friend, he said, "I've decided what I need to do. I'm going to get a job and *buy* Aunt Lucy that book."

"Very good, Mr. Brown," said Mr. Gruber. "Very good indeed."

CHAPTER 4
Paddington and the Close Shave

Paddington lost no time in looking for employment. He went into the first place that he saw on leaving Mr. Gruber's—Giuseppe's barber's shop.

"You are-a in-a luck!" cried the flamboyant Italian as Paddington set out his request. "I am in-a need of an assistant. I have-a much to do this afternoon. Please start by sweeping up-a. I shall be back in-a few-a minutes. *Ciao, ciao!*" And with that he threw Paddington a broom and left.

"*Ciao, ciao*, Giuseppe!" Paddington called after him.

He was about to set to and sweep up all the hair clippings when he spotted a white barber's coat hanging on the back of a door.

"It can't hurt to try it on," he said to himself. "After all, I may as well look the part."

Slipping out of his own coat, he took the barber's coat from the peg and put it on. Then he stood back and admired his new look in the mirror. Taking a comb, he parted his fur into a neat side parting.

"Ah, sir. Good afternoon," he said to his reflection, pretending to be a real barber. "Now, what can I do for you today?"

"Just a quick trim please," said a voice.

Paddington whirled round in surprise to see that a customer had walked in and was already installing himself in one of the barber's chairs. He was a large, pompous-looking man with a magnificent mane of gray hair.

"Come along, man, I haven't got all day," said the customer sharply.

"Oh, I—I'm not the barber," said Paddington. "I just tidy up."

"That's all I want," said the man, flicking his hand impatiently around his hair. "Tidy up at the back and sides and nothing off the top."

"Yes but—" Paddington began.

"No buts!" cried the man. "Come on, man. Chop, chop!" He settled back into the chair and immediately went to sleep, snoring softly.

"Chop, chop?" Paddington repeated. "If you say so, sir."

He fetched a cape and draped it over the sleeping man, then went to pick up some scissors. Unfortunately bears are not very good at holding scissors. Paddington found that out straightaway—his paws fumbled, the scissors slipped from his grasp and off they flew, out of his reach. They flew through the air like a dart and got stuck in one of the ceiling tiles.

Never one to give up, Paddington looked around for a different implement.

"I'll try the clippers instead," he said to himself.

The clippers were electric and had a long cable attached to them. Paddington went to a socket on the wall to plug them in; then he pressed the button on the clippers. To his horror, they were on such a high setting that the vibrations made him jump and judder around the room! He tried to make his way over to give the customer a trim, but began spinning in circles instead.

The cable on the clippers got caught in his legs. It began to wind itself tightly around him! Paddington was completely tangled up now. He was spinning round and round, totally out of control.

Just as things couldn't possibly get any worse, the phone rang. Paddington hopped over to answer it and knocked into a potted plant. It landed on his head. Anyone walking past would have seen a bear wearing a spiky green wig!

At last Paddington managed to reach the phone. He flipped it up with his mouth. The cable was still tight round his legs, and the juddering from the clippers made his voice rather shaky.

"G-g-g-good aft-t-t-ternoon. A c-c-cut and bl-bl-blow-dry, you s-s-s-ay? I'll have to ch-ch-ch-check the diary, b-b-but—" He stopped abruptly as he saw the electric cable had caught on the customer's seat. The man lurched sharply backward, still deeply asleep. At the same time Paddington was pulled paws-first straight toward the sleeping customer—and the clippers were aiming right at the back of the man's head!

"I sh-shall have to c-c-call you back," Paddington said in a panic. "I think I m-m-may be about to sh-sh-shave a c-c-customer . . ."

Just as he said this, the clippers connected with the man's hair and mowed a neat stripe right down the middle of his head.

"Oh!" cried Paddington.

He didn't have time to think, however, as the plug from the clippers had shot out of the wall socket and up into the air. Now it was caught in the ceiling fan! As the fan started whirring, faster and faster, Paddington struggled harder than ever to free himself. But he was tangled too tightly. Before he knew it, Paddington was pulled right up to the ceiling, spinning around at an alarmingly high speed.

Outside the shop, a mother and her little boy were having an argument.

"I don't want to!" the boy was shouting. "You can't make me!"

"Now you stop making a fuss, Nelson," the mother said sternly. "It's only a haircut. Nothing at all to be afraid of."

At that exact moment, Paddington was hurled against the window by the fan. He landed with a loud *SPLAT* against the glass, his eyes wide, his mouth open in panic. The plug was pulled from the socket by the force of the collision, and Paddington slid to the floor in a heap.

"I've changed my mind," said the woman, quickly turning her son to face the other way. "We'll go somewhere else."

Paddington picked himself up and went back to the customer. He gasped when he saw the strip shaved into the back of the man's head. It looked like a reverse Mohican!

What shall I do? Paddington wondered. He glanced at the pile of hair on the floor by the man's chair and had an idea. *I'll stick it back on,* he thought, bending down and scooping up the clippings. He patted them into place, but the shaved hair just fell to the floor again.

Paddington removed his hat to scratch his head while he thought what to do next. In so doing, he spotted the marmalade sandwich that he had placed there earlier. As he stared at it, another idea formed in his mind.

He scooped some marmalade out of the sandwich and

spread it on to the man's head and then picked up the hair clippings and stuck them on top. It was working rather well.

Paddington had stepped back to admire his handiwork when the customer stirred in his sleep.

"What are you doing?" the man mumbled.

"I thought you'd like some hair product, sir," said Paddington, thinking on his paws.

"Jolly good. Carry on," said the man, going back to sleep.

Paddington did as he was told.

At last, when he thought he could do no more for the customer, he shook him gently awake. "All done," he said. "Is sir happy with the trim?"

The man surveyed his reflection critically. "I suppose so," he said. "But what about the back?"

Paddington grabbed a hand mirror and fleetingly showed the customer the back of his head. The man frowned. He reached up and patted the marmalade-glued patch of hair.

"What's this?" he asked, puzzled.

"Marmalade, sir," said Paddington in a matter-of-fact tone. "Hairy marmalade," he added, thinking this sounded more the sort of product a barber might use.

"Hairy marmalade?" exclaimed the man. "Well, get it off!"

"Certainly, sir. Waste not, want not," said Paddington. He stretched up on the tips of his paws and leaned over to lick the marmalade off.

"WHAT-A ARE YOU DOING-A?" shouted a voice from the shop door.

"Ah, there you are, Mr. Giuseppe," said Paddington, glancing up. "This is not at all as bad as it looks," he added hastily when he took in the look of fury on the barber's face.

Giuseppe opened his mouth to reply that it was possibly a lot worse, but his words were drowned out by the deafening blare of the fire alarm.

Paddington looked up to see that sparks were flying out of the ceiling fan and smoke was filling the room! He looked around wildly for a way to stop the fire.

He need not have worried, for almost immediately some sprinklers came on, putting out the fire.

Unfortunately they also drenched everyone and Paddington decided that, under the circumstances, the best course of action was to beat a hasty retreat.

"I'm sorry, but I think perhaps working in a barber's shop is not my strongest suit," he cried on his way out. "*Ciao, ciao*, Giuseppe!"

CHAPTER 5

All the Fun of the Fair

That evening the Browns took the whole family to Madame Kozlova's Steam Fair as promised.

It certainly was a spectacular sight. Paddington didn't think he had seen anything as wonderful since leaving Darkest Peru. Judy and Jonathan were as excited as he was. They chattered away, pointing out the rides to Paddington and asking him which he would go on first. However, Paddington was deep in thought. He had not been able to take his mind off the pop-up book since seeing it in Mr. Gruber's shop and now that he was here, at the fair, he knew more than ever that he had to find a way of getting the book for Aunt Lucy. But how was he going to get another job after the disaster at the barber's? he wondered.

Mr. Brown had gone to buy some snacks. When he came back with cotton candy for Mrs. Bird and toffee apples for the others, Paddington asked Mr. Brown if he had ever been fired from a job.

Mr. Brown looked uncomfortable. "Not exactly, but . . . I think you should be careful about entering the workplace, Paddington. Are you sure you're ready? It's a tough, competitive world out there, and I should know," he added wearily. "I worry that a kind good-natured bear like you might get trampled underfoot."

Paddington considered this as he took a bite from a toffee apple.

"Dad's right," said Judy, suddenly sullen. "You can't trust anyone."

Paddington tried to open his mouth to protest that this wasn't true—he knew he could trust the Browns, for example—but he found the toffee apple had glued his teeth together, so he remained silent.

Mrs. Brown put a hand on Judy's shoulder. "Is this about Tony, darling?" she asked.

"No," Judy snapped.

"Everything's about *Tony*," Jonathan teased.

"At least I'm not pretending to be someone I'm not," Judy retaliated.

"Nor am I," said Jonathan irritably. He moved away from his sister toward a group of boys who all appeared to be dressed in a similar fashion with cyber-shades and baseball caps. "Hey, G-Man!" Jonathan cried, slipping on his own shades and performing a complicated hand gesture.

"J-Dog," said the boy, walking over in a slouch, one hand raised. "Spud bounce, man," he said, bumping his fist against Jonathan's.

Paddington had finally managed to work his mouth free of the toffee. "But, Mr. Brown," he said, continuing the conversation from before, "I'm sure I will be fine in the workplace. Aunt Lucy said if you're kind and polite, all will be right."

"Someone's making sense at last," said Mrs. Bird. She gave Jonathan and his friend a funny look.

"*You* are kind and polite, Mr. Brown," Paddington went on. "And you've made it to the top."

Mr. Brown grimaced. "I'm nowhere near the top, Paddington. I peaked in the middle. And now my hair's going gray and my belly has popped out and I creak."

Mrs. Brown took her husband's arm. "You don't creak, darling," she said. "When do you creak?"

"When I sit down. When I get up . . . ," said Mr. Brown.

"I thought that was the chair," said Mrs. Brown kindly.

"Nope," Mr. Brown said, looking miserable.

Just then there was a burst of applause from the crowd and the family turned to see a handsome man bounce onto the stage in front of them. "Oh!" cried Paddington. "Doesn't that man live in the big house on the corner of Windsor Gardens?"

"Yes," said Judy, taking a photo. "He's one of dad's celebrity clients—Phoenix Buchanan."

Mr. Brown nodded importantly. "He's a Platinum Club member and a very famous actor."

"Or used to be," said Mrs. Bird knowingly. "Now he does dog-food commercials."

Mrs. Brown smiled. "Mrs. Bird doesn't like him, Paddington, because he can never remember her name."

"That's not the only reason . . . ," muttered Mrs. Bird.

Paddington saw that behind the man there was a banner that read: "Kozlova's Steam Fair—Where All Your Dreams Come True."

Just like the line on the cover of the pop-up book, Paddington thought dreamily. *If only I could find a way of getting enough money to buy it for Aunt Lucy—then her dreams would come true as well.*

His thoughts were interrupted by Phoenix Buchanan's voice ringing out from the stage.

"Thank you. Oh please, stop it!" the actor was saying as the crowd continued to clap and cheer. He flapped his hands coyly, pretending to be embarrassed by the attention. The applause petered out and Phoenix cried, "No, no, please carry on . . . Oh, what am I like?" he simpered.

"I'm at my absolute *naughtiest* tonight. I'm tickled to the deepest shade of *shrimp* to open this wonderful old steam fair." The crowd cheered. "But let me tell you," Phoenix went on, "when Madame Kozlova created it years ago she didn't do it for the likes of *me*—'celebrity,' 'star of stage and screen' (I hate all that stuff, honest I do). 'West End legend'—there's another one. Ha-ha! No, she made it for the *ordinary* guys, like *you* lot." He pointed at the audience. "And that's why I'd like to ask one of *you* to come up here and help start things off. Any volunteers?" he asked, surveying the crowd.

Paddington's paw shot up. "Bears are good at volunteering," he said.

Phoenix looked out at the sea of hands. "Let me see . . . Eeny, meeny, miny—bear?" he said, looking puzzled as he spotted Paddington. "Yes, why not?" he said. "What about you, young ursine? Come on up." He beckoned to Paddington to join him as the audience clapped.

"And you are . . . ?" Phoenix asked.

"Paddington Brown," said Paddington, raising his hat.

"Of course you are!" exclaimed Phoenix. "You're my next-door neighbor." He beamed. "You live with Henry and Mary and Mrs.—er—Fuh-Nuh-Nuh," he mumbled.

"You mean Mrs. Bird," said Paddington helpfully.

"That's the one," said Phoenix dismissively. "More

importantly, do you know who *I* am?" He pointed to himself and winked at the crowd.

"You're a very famous actor," said Paddington.

"Oh, blah!" said Phoenix, fluttering his eyelashes with false modesty.

"Or used to be . . ." Paddington went on. "Now you do dog-food commercials."

A snigger ran through the crowd and Phoenix's smile faded. "Well, a man has to eat," he said.

"What, dog food?" Paddington asked, puzzled.

The crowd erupted into laughter and Phoenix forced a laugh along with them. "Ha-ha! Very funny." He paused and became dramatically serious and mysterious. "Enough of me . . . They say that at Kozlova's 'all your dreams come true.' Did you know that, young bear? If you could have one wish come true tonight, what would it be?"

"That's easy," said Paddington. "I'd like to get Aunt Lucy a birthday present."

"Aww!" Phoenix gushed, clutching his hands together. "How sweet!"

"Yes, I've had my eye on an old pop-up book of London," Paddington explained. "Made by Madame Kozlova's great-grandmother, as it happens."

Phoenix's eyes lit up at this bit of information. He quickly tried to hide his interest. "Really?" he said carelessly. "How . . . fascinating."

"Yes, just as soon as I saw it I knew Aunt Lucy would love it," said Paddington.

"Well, I'm not sure I could promise you that," said Phoenix. "But . . ." He faced the crowd and raised his voice. "I *can* promise you will all have oodles of fun, darlings! So, if you'll lend me a paw, Paddington, I'd like to declare Madame Kozlova's Steam Fair OPEN!"

Paddington put his paw on top of Phoenix's hand and together they pulled a lever. Immediately the old fairground organ sprang to life. Paddington stared in awe as thousands of light bulbs flicked on around the fair and the magnificent old steam rides started moving. The horses spun round and round and up and down on the carousel, the swing-boats began swinging, and the ghost train let out a stream of spooky noises. Paddington couldn't wait to go and explore.

He was about to set off to find the Browns again when Phoenix Buchanan took him to one side.

"Young bear! Young bear! A word in your ear. This pop-up book," said the actor, looking around to check that no one was listening in.

"Do you know it?" asked Paddington.

"I know *of* it," said Phoenix, "but I was led to believe it was lost. Where on earth did *you* find it?"

Not picking up on the eagerness in Phoenix's voice,

Paddington replied, "I saw it in Mr. Gruber's antique shop on the Portobello Road. He's keeping it to one side for me, but it's very expensive. I don't suppose *you* have any advice about making money, do you?" he asked hopefully.

"Not really, no," said Phoenix. He was losing interest in talking to Paddington now and rather wanted to get rid of him, as a plan was forming in his mind. "I suppose you'll just have to start at the bottom of the ladder and work your way up," he added hurriedly, before turning away.

Paddington's eyes lit up. "Do you know what, Mr. Buchanan? You've given me a brilliant idea!"

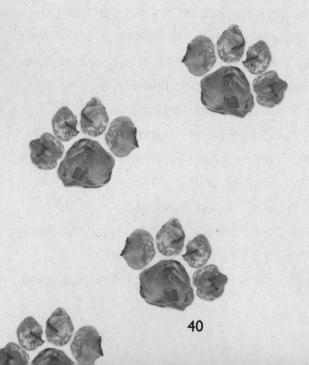

CHAPTER 6

Paddington Cleans Up

Phoenix's comment about starting "at the bottom of the ladder" had got Paddington thinking. The residents of Windsor Gardens had been saying for some time that they needed to find a new window cleaner. The morning after the steam fair, Paddington announced that he was the bear for the job.

"I have always fancied a job that involved heights," he told them. "In Darkest Peru I was very good at climbing trees."

He asked Mr. Brown if he could use an old telescopic ladder he had found in the basement. "It will fit into my suitcase beautifully," he explained. "I'll have every window in the street cleaned by the end of the day."

Surely this will earn me enough money to buy that book for Aunt Lucy, he thought as he went on his way.

Mr. Brown watched Paddington go down the street with a bucket, some soap and cloths, and the telescopic ladder folded into his suitcase. "Are we sure that bear knows what he is doing?" he said.

"Oh, darling, you worry too much," said Mrs. Brown, patting his arm.

Paddington had decided to start at Dr. Jafri's house. He extended his ladder and propped it up against the wall, then filled the bucket with water from an outside tap and squirted soap into it. He intended to climb the ladder with the bucket and start cleaning from the top floor down.

However, when Paddington went to pick up the bucket, he found it was so heavy he couldn't lift it off the ground. He stopped and considered the situation, then went to his suitcase to see if there was anything of use in it. He found a length of rope and also a marmalade sandwich. The latter proved very fortifying, and once he had finished it he knew what he should do. He took the rope and tied it to the bucket. Then, taking the other end of the rope with him, he climbed the ladder and fed the other end of rope behind a drainpipe attached to the wall. Then he closed his eyes and jumped off the ladder.

Paddington immediately went whizzing down on the rope at top speed and then—*CLUNK!* He stopped suddenly, his feet dangling in midair. He opened his eyes to find that he was dangling halfway between the ground and the top of the ladder.

"Oh dear. I'm too light," he said, wondering how he could make himself heavy enough to reach the ground. Then he spotted a flowerpot on a window ledge. "That will do!" he said, grabbing it.

Sure enough, he was now the correct weight. The bucket went up and Paddington went down.

Feeling rather pleased with himself, Paddington took off his hat with his free hand and used it to mop his brow. Then he put the hat to one side and looked up.

Now the bucket was coming down again at top speed!

"Oh no! My hat was the only thing making me heavier than the bucket!" Paddington cried.

The bucket descended so fast that before Paddington could do anything to prevent it, it fell smack on to his head, emptying its contents all over him.

"Ow!" cried Paddington.

He removed the bucket and wiped the soapy water from his eyes.

From inside the house Dr. Jafri had seen the whole thing. His windows were now covered in soapy water. He looked puzzled, as there was a sudden enthusiastic movement behind the bubbles and Paddington's face came into view.

"Sorry, Dr. Jafri!" Paddington called. He was using his furry body to wipe the glass! "There you are—all clean now."

Dr. Jafri smiled and shook his head indulgently. "Thank you, Paddington," he said, opening a window to hand the bear some coins.

"Thank *you*, Dr. Jafri," said Paddington eagerly. "I think I'm getting the hang of cleaning windows now."

Paddington decided to try the Colonel's house next. He rang the bell.

"Good morning, Colonel," he said, raising his hat. "Would you like your windows cleaned for a bargain price?"

"Go away!" said the grumpy Colonel.

"Are you sure?" said Paddington. "They're awfully dirty. I'm surprised you can see out of them at all."

"I can't," said the Colonel. "And I don't care and I'm certainly not paying *you*." He slammed the door in Paddington's face.

Paddington decided he would clean them anyway. He couldn't believe that the Colonel really didn't care about his windows being so dirty.

The Colonel stomped back inside his gloomy house and made himself a cup of tea.

"Bears cleaning windows?" he muttered to himself. "Whatever next?"

But as he said this, Paddington finished the first pane of glass and warm sunlight flooded the room for the first time in years. The Colonel went to look out on to the street and saw Miss Kitts, who waved up at him shyly. The Colonel waved tentatively back.

DING-DONG!

The Colonel jumped. "Two house calls in one day?" he grumbled. "It's like Piccadilly Circus here this morning."

The Colonel opened the door to see Mr. Curry on the doorstep. Mr. Curry was the Browns' irritable next-door neighbor. He had taken a dislike to Paddington the moment he had met him. Nothing the bear had done since had changed Mr. Curry's opinion of him. Today the nosy neighbor was wearing a florescent jacket and hat and carrying a clipboard. He had a megaphone attached to his belt and was looking even more pleased with himself than normal.

"Good afternoon, Colonel," said Mr. Curry. "Are you aware there is a *bear* on your roof?"

"Yes, I am," said the Colonel. "He's cleaning my windows."

"Hello, Mr. Curry!" Paddington shouted down. He was on the top floor now. "Would you like me to clean your gutters while I'm up here, Colonel?"

The Colonel looked up and smiled. "Yes, please, Paddington."

Mr. Curry looked disappointed. "Well, it's not for me to say, sir, but *I* certainly wouldn't care to have a wild animal climbing all over the place. And as commander of your Community Defense Force—"

"Is that an *official* position, Mr. Curry?" the Colonel interrupted. "Or have you just bought a yellow coat?"

Mr. Curry looked affronted. He opened his mouth to reply, but before he could get a word out a large clod of dirt landed on his head.

"Whoops!" said Paddington. He had dislodged the muck from the Colonel's gutter.

The Colonel smiled up at him and shut the door in Mr. Curry's face.

CHAPTER 7

Stop, Thief!

Paddington was very tired. He had spent several long days doing odd jobs now. He had washed windows up and down the city—he had even startled Mr. Brown by tapping on his top-floor office window while cleaning! Paddington was now walking home at the end of another very busy day with a suitcase full of coins from satisfied customers.

He passed by Mr. Gruber's shop and stopped to peer in through the window at the pop-up book.

"If I have one more day like today, I shall have enough money for your present, Aunt Lucy," he said to himself.

He was about to go on his way when he heard the sound of breaking glass. He looked up and spotted a shadowy figure climbing in through a second-floor window.

"Mr. Gruber?" Paddington called up. "Have you locked yourself out like Dr. Jafri?" He peered at the figure and saw it wasn't Mr. Gruber, but a strange man with a beard.

It took a second for the penny to drop, and then

Paddington cried, "Thief!"

"Lawks!" cried the thief, and he disappeared in through the window.

"Oh, no you don't!" shouted Paddington, setting his window-cleaning ladder up against the wall and scurrying up.

But he was too late; the thief was already inside and running downstairs to the antiques shop below. Before Paddington could reach him, the thief had smashed the display case, snatched the pop-up book, and run out of the front door.

"Stop, thief!" Paddington shouted, running out of the shop after him, just as the burglar alarm went off.

As Paddington ran after the man, a police car pulled up outside Mr. Gruber's. A policewoman grabbed her radio and spoke into it urgently. "Robbery in progress at Gruber's Antiques. The suspect is a . . . small bear in a red hat and duffle coat." She jumped out of her car and chased after Paddington, who was himself chasing the thief down the road to the canal.

Paddington came out onto the towpath just in time to see the thief take a bike from the top of a boat and make off with it.

Paddington put his paw in his mouth and whistled. A large dog appeared.

"Wolfie!" Paddington cried with relief. "You're just

in time!"

"Woof!" Wolfie replied.

Paddington jumped onto the dog's back, riding him like a horse in pursuit of the thief.

"Come back with that book!" Paddington shouted. He could see it poking out of the bike's pannier. "Faster, Wolfie!" he cried.

Wolfie picked up speed and Paddington almost got close enough to the bike to take the book, but the thief saw him and snatched it out of the pannier. He pedaled faster than ever, veering off sharply across a bridge and leaving Paddington and Wolfie behind on the other side of the canal.

Wolfie was not going to let the thief go that easily. He spotted a shortcut and jumped on to the roof of a boat with Paddington clinging on to his fur. The pair leaped across the water on to an island in the middle of the canal and disappeared into the undergrowth together.

When Paddington came out the other side, Wolfie was nowhere to be seen but Paddington was holding on to the legs of an enormous swan! It swooped up into the sky, chasing after the thief once more.

The thief looked up, yelped in surprise, lost control of the bike, and fell off. The bike veered off course and dropped like a stone into the murky water.

"Come back!" Paddington shouted. "That book is

reserved for Aunt Lucy!" But he could only watch in vain as the thief continued his getaway on foot. "Thank you for the lift," he said to the swan, spotting Wolfie on the towpath below. "If you could just drop me off here, that would be splendid!"

The swan set Paddington down on the path next to Wolfie and the pair chased the thief all the way to the newspaper kiosk in Windsor Gardens.

Hearing police sirens coming from the other direction, the thief stopped. He was cornered, and he knew it.

"All right, all right! You got me!" he cried, raising his hands. He was still holding the pop-up book.

Paddington jumped down from Wolfie's back and approached the thief. "Hand over the book!" he commanded.

But the thief was not going to give up his booty that easily. "'Fraid I can't do that," he said with a cheeky grin. "Cheerio!" Then he turned and DISAPPEARED IN A PUFF OF SMOKE!

Paddington stood, staring openmouthed at the space where the thief had been. He looked around wildly— the man must be somewhere. Then the policewoman appeared behind him. She had caught up at last.

"Hold it right there," she said to Paddington, coming toward him.

Paddington breathed a sigh of relief. "Thank goodness

you're here," he said with a smile. "I was trying to stop a thief—"

The policewoman held up a finger, however, and prevented him from saying any more. "Put your paws in the air," she demanded.

"But *I'm* not the thief!" Paddington protested, horrified. "The thief was right here. You just missed him, in fact. He—he . . ." Paddington didn't know how to explain what he had just witnessed.

"I suppose you're going to tell me that he disappeared in a puff of smoke?" said the policewoman sarcastically.

"Well, yes," said Paddington. "That's exactly what happened actually."

Unfortunately, the policewoman was not impressed with Paddington's explanation. She took some handcuffs from her belt and slapped them on to his paws. "I think you'd better come with me, young bear," she said, and with that she took him back to Windsor Gardens.

The neighbors were watching at their windows when the police car drew up outside 32 Windsor Gardens. The Browns rushed out in a panic.

Mrs. Brown tried to hug him. "Paddington! We were so worried about you."

"Are you all right?" asked Judy.

"Where have you been?" asked Jonathan.

"He was caught red-pawed robbing Gruber's Antiques," said the policewoman.

"No!" said Paddington. "I told you—it wasn't me."

"Now, listen here," Mr. Brown said to the policewoman. "There must be some mistake."

"No mistake, sir," the policewoman answered. "Like I said, I caught him in the act."

Mr. Curry had come out of his house, a sly smile on his face. He had heard every word. "Well, well. The truth will out," he said. "We opened our hearts to that bear. We opened our doors—well, *you* did," he said to the Browns, "I kept mine triple-locked in accordance with the community neighborhood watch guidelines— and all along he was robbing you blind. I hate to say I told you so, but I definitely *did* tell you so."

The other neighbors were out in the street too now, muttering to each other.

"Can this be true?" asked Dr. Jafri.

"Paddington, a thief?" said Miss Kitts.

"We'll be taking him to the station," the policewoman told the Browns. "You'll be hearing from us in due course." And with that Paddington was put inside a police van and driven away.

Mrs. Brown sobbed as she watched him go, his little

face pressed to the glass, a picture of fear and shame.

Meanwhile, in an attic room, the bearded thief was sitting in front of a theatrical makeup mirror and talking to himself in a gruff London accent.

"A nice little haul and no mistake," he said as he pulled off his beard—and his nose! "Turned out to be quite a stroke of luck, that bear turning up when he did. Coppers think he done it, and now we're in the clear."

With one last tug, the rest of the disguise was off, revealing that the thief was, in fact, none other than Phoenix Buchanan, the actor that Paddington had spoken to at the steam fair!

"Yes, Magwitch," he said to his reflection in his normal voice. "We gave quite a performance, you and I—just like the old days."

Phoenix's attic room was full of mannequins of all the characters he had played over the years. He got up from his makeup table and strutted around, talking to them all.

Catching sight of a mannequin dressed in black with a skull in its hand, he asked it, "Why the lemon face, Hamlet? If you have something to say, please share it with us all."

Then, putting on a Shakespearean voice, Phoenix answered as Hamlet. "It is not nor it cannot come to good."

Continuing as himself he said, "Oh, you and your dreary

conscience, Hamlet. Tell me this—what would you prefer? That you sit here gathering dust while I humiliate myself in a spaniel costume, or that we all return in glory with the greatest one-man show the West End has ever seen?"

Phoenix began bowing and smiling as he imagined applause from a large audience.

"I know what *you're* thinking, Scrooge," he said to another mannequin. "It'll cost a fortune to put on such a show. But if I'm right, that's exactly what this book will provide." He waved the pop-up book triumphantly. "All I have to do is follow the little lady in the pictures to each of the landmarks in London and look for the clues she has left me. Once I have all the clues, the hidden Kozlova treasure will be mine!"

He peered closely at the first page of the book. "There she is," he said. "Hello!" He waved at the figure of a tiny trapeze artist. She had been drawn as though she were balancing on a walkway on Tower Bridge directly over a coat of arms.

"So *that* is where the treasure hunt begins, is it?" Phoenix said with glee. "Tower Bridge . . . I wonder what disguise I should use for this little escapade?"

He glanced around the room and his eyes settled on a suit of armor.

"That'll do nicely," he said.

CHAPTER 8

Paddington and the Long Arm of the Law

All too soon it was the date of Paddington's trial. He was standing in the dock, feeling so nervous he was sure the whole courtroom could hear his knees knocking together. Would the jury believe that he was innocent and that someone else had broken into Mr. Gruber's shop? He hoped that Mr. Gruber would say all the right things and that he would soon be going home to 32 Windsor Gardens. He looked up sorrowfully and saw the Browns and his friends and neighbors looking down at him from the gallery.

"He looks so tiny," said Mrs. Brown anxiously.

"And confused and afraid," added Mr. Brown.

"Try not to worry," said Dr. Jafri. He smiled in what he hoped was a reassuring manner. "We all know that Paddington is innocent. His name is sure to be cleared."

"And Mr. Gruber will speak up for him," said Miss Kitts. She patted Mrs. Brown's arm.

Paddington couldn't make out what they were all saying, but he saw from Mrs. Brown's face that she was worried. He didn't like to think that it was him who had caused her so much anxiety. He told himself to stay positive and that soon she and the rest of the family would be smiling and happy again.

"Deep breath, Paddington," he said to himself. "Remember what Mr. Brown said—you're young, you've done nothing wrong, you'll be fine. So long as you get a fair-minded judge."

The judge suddenly called out, "Order! Order!" All the murmured conversations in the courtroom ceased and everyone rose to their feet. Paddington crossed his claws, hoping that Mr. Brown was right. But as soon as he looked up and saw the judge's face he feared all hope was lost. It was the same man who had come into Giuseppe's barber's shop on that fateful morning! He was unlikely to be well disposed toward Paddington after the incident with the clippers and the hairy marmalade.

"Oh dear," said Paddington under his breath. *Perhaps he won't recognize me*, he thought.

If the annoyed look on the judge's face was anything to go by, however, it would seem that he very much *had* recognized Paddington. "Quiet!" he roared. "We will now hear the case of the Crown versus Paddington Brown."

The crown prosecutor called Mr. Gruber to the stand. The old antiques dealer glanced across at Paddington and flashed him a brief smile.

Paddington willed his friend to say all the right things. *Come on, Mr. Gruber,* he thought. *If anyone can persuade the judge of my innocence, it's you.*

"Mr. Gruber," said the prosecutor. "Would you say the defendant had a particular interest in the pop-up book?"

"Oh yes, he loved the book," said Mr. Gruber, smiling eagerly. "I would say that he had his heart set right on top of it."

Mrs. Brown sighed and bit her lip. That was not an answer that was likely to do Paddington any favors, she thought.

The prosecutor went on. "So, you discussed how expensive the book was?"

"Ye-es," said Mr. Gruber. He paused as he realized the direction in which the questioning was going, and then he said, "But Paddington was earning the money to buy it. I refuse to believe that young Paddington Brown would ever burglarize my shop."

Mr. Brown squeezed his wife's hand and she gave him a brave smile. Mr. Gruber's evidence was very helpful to Paddington's case, but the next person called to the stand was a forensic investigator.

"Paw prints were found here"—the investigator was pointing to a plan of Mr. Gruber's shop—"here . . . and here. And a substance, later identified as *marmalade*, was found here."

The prosecutor opened a jar. "And this is the same marmalade?" he asked.

"That's mine!" Mrs. Bird hissed. "How did they get hold of that, I'd like to know?"

The forensic investigator dipped a finger in and tasted the marmalade. "Yes, it is."

There was a murmur of voices in the gallery. Paddington looked up at the noise. He was horrified to see the expressions on people's faces. The marmalade evidence had not gone down well—it seemed that several of Paddington's neighbors were beginning to be swayed against him.

Finally Phoenix Buchanan was asked to take the stand.

Paddington relaxed slightly. Mr. Buchanan was a friendly neighbor and he had been very kind to Paddington at the fair. Surely he would convince the jury that they had got the wrong bear?

The actor took the stand, flashing a grin at the jury, clearing enjoying being the center of attention. There was some giggling and people whispered behind their hands as they recognized who Phoenix was.

The clerk called for silence. "Phoenix Buchanan," he said. "Do you swear to tell the truth, the whole truth, and nothing but the truth?"

"I do," said Phoenix, putting on an exaggeratedly serious tone. "May my entrails be plucked forth and wound about my neck should I deceive." Then, turning to the gallery, he gave a cheeky smile and added, "Prison is no laughing matter. And I should know. I spent three years in *Les Misérables*."

The courtroom erupted into delighted laughter. Phoenix certainly knew how to turn a crowd to his advantage.

The counsel for the prosecution stood and addressed the actor. "Mr. Buchanan, you live on the same street as the defendant?"

"I do," said Phoenix.

The prosecutor nodded. "And you were an eyewitness to the events that night?"

"Indeed I was," Phoenix replied, all seriousness and formality again. "I was up late when I became aware of a hullabaloo on the street below. I went to my awards room, which is a *large* room that overlooks the newspaper kiosk," he added, looking around the room for a reaction. There was no response, so he continued. "And I saw Paddington riding a rather disreputable-looking hound."

The prosecutor handed Phoenix a drawing of the thief. "Mary Brown drew this based on the bear's description of the man he claims he was chasing. Did you see him on the street that night?"

Phoenix took the drawing. "Well, let me see," he said, stroking his chin. "Hmm. Handsome devil, isn't he? Dazzling eyes—"

"Yes," the prosecutor interrupted. "But did you see him? Your answer will tell us whether the bear is guilty. Did you see this man?"

Phoenix raised his eyes and looked at Paddington, then gazing around the courtroom sorrowfully he answered, "Alas, I did not."

The court descended into uproar.

"Silence!" roared the judge, banging his gavel.

Phoenix stepped slowly down from the stand, avoiding Paddington's horrified stare.

This isn't possible, Paddington thought. *How can this be happening?*

He looked up at the Browns. Mrs. Brown had tears in her eyes and Mr. Brown had his head in his hands. Mrs. Bird was the only one who had an expression of fiery determination on her face.

"I don't trust that man," she muttered. "I've never trusted actors."

CHAPTER 9

The Hunt Is On

Later that night, while poor Paddington was being led away to Portobello Prison to start his sentence, Phoenix was plotting the next phase of his wicked plan.

He had taken his suit of armor from his attic room and was on his way to Tower Bridge, where he believed the first of the clues to be hidden.

"I am going to get my hands on that treasure and then I shall be able to kiss the world of dog-food commercials goodbye once and for all!" he said to himself as he approached the North Tower of Tower Bridge.

He ducked behind a pillar when he saw that a security guard was doing his rounds, and quickly changed into the suit of armor.

The guard walked past, shining his torch ahead of him as he went. As soon as he had gone, a visor opened on one of the suits of armor—it was, of course, the one with Phoenix Buchanan inside. His disguise had worked every bit as well as his thief's costume, and the guard had not suspected a thing!

The actor waited until the coast was clear, and then he ran awkwardly in the armor to a large Gothic window. Heaving it open, he climbed out on to an elevated walkway. The dark waters of the Thames swirled below. Taking a deep breath, Phoenix edged along the walkway to the coat of arms in the middle of the bridge, where the tiny trapeze artist had been standing in the picture in the pop-up book.

He leaned over. "Now, where is that clue?" he said to himself as he scanned the stonework. "Aha!" He had caught sight of something—a letter carved into the back of the coat of arms. "The letter 'D'!" He fished inside his disguise for a notebook and pencil and jotted the letter down. "The hunt is on!" he said with a nasty smile. "Soon the treasure will be mine."

Paddington was not having so much luck. His appeal to the judge's better nature had not worked and Phoenix's last comment had sealed his fate as far as the jury were concerned. They had found him guilty. He now found himself in prison, wearing a gray striped uniform and prisoner's cap.

"Paddington Brown?" said a stern warden, handing him a rolled-up blanket.

Paddington gulped and nodded. "Yes, sir," he said.

"Ten years for grand theft," the warden said, looking at his notes. "And grievous barberly harm." He raised an eyebrow and looked back up at Paddington. "Follow me."

A buzzer sounded and a barred door slid open. Paddington followed the warden into the prison atrium and up some stairs to the cells. They went along a walkway until the warden stopped outside a door. He unlocked it and Paddington stepped inside. The cell was very gloomy indeed. There was one narrow bed and a tiny window that was too high up for Paddington to see out of. He suddenly felt incredibly homesick for his little attic room at 32 Windsor Gardens.

"The Browns usually read me a story before I go to bed," Paddington said to the warden. "I don't suppose—"

"Sorry, son," said the warden firmly. "No bedtime stories here." And with that he closed the door firmly behind him, locked it, and walked away.

Paddington climbed on to the bed and settled down to write a letter to his aunt. He had promised he would write regularly—he couldn't let going to prison get in the way of that. He decided, however, that he couldn't face telling Aunt Lucy the whole truth, so he did his best to put a positive spin on things.

Dear Aunt Lucy,

A great deal has happened since I last wrote. There's been a bit of a mix-up with your present and the upshot is I've had to leave Windsor Gardens and move . . . somewhere else. It's not quite as charming as the Browns' house, but it's not at all bad. It's a period property—in fact, it's one of the most substantial Victorian buildings in London. And the security arrangements are second to none.

I'm only allowed to see the Browns once a month. I wonder what they're doing now? I hope they don't forget me. I hope they'll sort everything out and I'll be able to go home and get your present and everything will be as right as rain. I just need to hold on until then.

All my love,

Padingtun

Paddington need not have worried. Of course the Browns had not forgotten him. They were extremely worried and were doing everything they could think of to prove his innocence.

Mrs. Brown was already hot on the case; she had given her drawing of the thief to Judy, who had made it up into a poster with the heading "Have you seen this man?" Mrs. Brown was determined to put copies up all around

London in a bid to catch the real thief.

She went first to Mr. Gruber and asked if she could put up a poster in his shop.

"Somebody's got to recognize him sooner or later," said Mrs. Brown as she fixed the picture to the glass on the front door.

"Hmm," said Mr. Gruber. He was deep in thought and didn't appear to be listening.

Mrs. Brown turned back to face him. "Are you all right, Mr. Gruber?" she asked with a frown.

Mr. Gruber scratched his head. "There's something about this whole business that's been tickling my brain-box," he said thoughtfully.

"What is it?" Mrs. Brown asked. She took a sketch-pad out of her bag and pulled a pencil from her hair, poised and ready for any information Mr. Gruber could offer.

Mr. Gruber began to speak slowly and carefully. "On the night of the robbery. When young Mr. Brown called out, the thief took to his heels and ran downstairs . . ."

Mrs. Brown imagined the thief running through Mr. Gruber's flat. ". . . and he came straight through the shop," she said, continuing Mr. Gruber's train of thought, "and out the front doors, setting off the alarm."

Mr. Gruber cut in. "Ah, but that's the thing," he said,

wagging his finger, "he *didn't* go straight through the shop."

Mrs. Brown looked puzzled. "No?" she said.

Mr. Gruber shook his head. "He came all the way over here," he said, gesturing to the back of the shop, "to get the popping book. Why not take some jewelry or a vase? They're much closer and far more valuable."

Mrs. Brown's eyes widened as she saw what Mr. Gruber was saying. "Oh!" she said.

"He can't know much about antiques," said Mr. Gruber, looking unimpressed.

"No . . . ," Mrs. Brown agreed. "Unless he knew something about that book that we don't."

They exchanged a glance as the same idea dawned on them both—the book must contain some kind of very valuable secret.

And I intend to find it out, Mrs. Brown thought to herself. Whatever the secret is, it will be sure to prove the thief's motive for stealing the book—and that Paddington is innocent beyond doubt!

CHAPTER 10

It All Comes Out in the Wash

Paddington certainly was not finding it easy, settling into prison life. Nevertheless, he had decided to make the best of a bad situation. He was going to do everything he could to fit in with the other prisoners, he told himself as he followed them out of the atrium that morning.

And I must remember my manners, he thought. *Aunt Lucy says it's important to always be kind and polite. That will be sure to make me friends.*

As soon as he had formed his resolution, however, he came face-to-face with a rather scary-looking tattooed prisoner. Paddington took a deep breath and reminded himself of Aunt Lucy's advice.

He looked the terrifying prisoner in the eye and, raising his prison uniform cap, he said, "Good morning. I'm Paddington Brown. How do you do?"

"Very funny. Ha-ha," said the man sarcastically. "I'm T-Bone. And you'd better stay out of my way."

67

"Oh, so I take it you won't be interested in setting up a gardening club with me?" Paddington persisted.

T-Bone glared at him. "And I take it you won't be interested in being buried in a deep, dark hole?" he snarled.

Paddington most certainly wasn't interested in that at all, so he decided it was best to remain silent.

"There you are," said the warden, coming along the line to Paddington. "Brown, P.—laundry duty," he said, ticking Paddington's name off a list of jobs.

Well, that doesn't sound too bad, thought Paddington. *What could possibly go wrong on laundry duty?*

Paddington found his way down to the prison laundry room. There were four machines, each clearly labeled: "Bedding," "Towels," "Uniforms," and "Colors."

"This seems simple enough," Paddington said to himself. "I've seen Mrs. Bird do this at home, so I'm sure I can cope."

He went over to a laundry chute and pulled it open. Right away an avalanche of dirty linen fell out of the chute, landing on top of his head and burying him. He burrowed his way out and began loading the clothes into the machine marked "Uniforms." He poured in the detergent, closed the door and pressed "Start."

"There," he said, feeling pleased with himself. "Nothing to do now except sit back and wait."

He took a step away from the machine and was about to sit down when, as the wash cycle began, Paddington noticed something going round and round with the prisoners' uniforms. Something that should not have been in there. Something small and red.

It was a single red sock.

"No!" Paddington cried. "Mrs. Bird always says you should never put colors on a hot wash!"

He pushed all the buttons in a frenzy, trying unsuccessfully to stop the cycle. Then in desperation he tried to open the door.

The water was turning an ominous light pink . . .

Paddington tugged and tugged at the handle on the door, but it appeared to be locked fast. He tried to remain calm.

"It's only *one* red sock," he told himself. "What's the worst that could happen?"

As if in answer to his question, the door handle suddenly snapped off in Paddington's paw. He was thrown backward on to the floor, just as the water turned a very dark shade of pink indeed.

The new look did not go down at all well with the

prison inmates. Later that day in the canteen Paddington found himself surrounded by a bunch of hardened criminals all decked out in bright pink uniforms. The men glared dangerously at Paddington.

"Afternoon, chaps," Paddington said as breezily as he could. "If you ask me, the pink brightens the place up a bit." He swallowed as he saw T-Bone separate himself from the crowd.

The big scary man leaned toward the little bear, his face inches from Paddington's. "If you ask me, Bear, you should pipe down and eat your dinner, because it might be your last."

"Okay," said Paddington. He was quaking as he turned and walked toward a table, his tray rattling in his paws.

He found a vacant spot, raised his cap shakily to the prisoners on either side of him, and looked down at his meal. It was a disgusting slop of gray sludge. He sniffed at it to try to work out what it was and recoiled in horror.

"Urgh!" he said.

A friendly-looking Australian who introduced himself as Phibs told him not to worry about the food. "It's not as bad as it looks," he said. "And I should know—I used to be a restaurant critic."

Paddington took heart from this and smiled. "Okay," he said, trying a spoonful. He immediately spat it back out again and looked sorrowfully at Phibs.

"I say it's not as bad as it looks," Phibs said with a grin, "because it's *worse*, isn't it, Spoon?" he said to a man who was making a model of a windmill with matchsticks.

The man nodded.

"What *is* this?" Paddington asked.

Spoon shrugged as he added another matchstick to his model. "Nobody knows," he said glumly.

His neighbor, a man with a mustache, piped up, "But we've been eating it three times a day for the last ten years."

Paddington looked shocked at this. "Why doesn't someone have a word with the chef? If he knew you all hated it, he might think about changing the menu."

A dozy-looking prisoner dropped his mug in surprise. "Have a word with the chef?" he repeated. "Knuckles, you mean?"

Spoon shuddered and shot Paddington a warning glance. "Two things to remember, if you want to survive in here, mate: keep your head down and *never* talk to Knuckles."

Paddington considered this piece of advice seriously. "Thank you," he said. "I will remember that."

But T-Bone's eyes had lit up during this conversation. "Actually," he said, "I think it's a great idea. The bear could have a little chat with Knuckles on our behalf."

Paddington looked at the other men's faces. They looked doubtful. "Do you really think that would work, Mr. T-Bone?" Paddington asked.

T-Bone nodded enthusiastically. "Tell you what, son, you have a word with Knuckles about him changing the menu, and we might forget about you turning *us* into a bunch of flamingos." He jabbed at his bright pink uniform and gave Paddington a distinctly nasty smile.

Paddington didn't notice T-Bone's expression, though. He was so keen on the prospect of making the peace that he was willing to try anything. He wanted nothing more than to be on good terms with everyone. "All right, then," he said. "I'll talk to him!"

He got up and began looking around for the chef. Knuckles wasn't hard to spot: firstly because he was wearing a chef's apron and secondly because he was a mountain of a man. He was so huge that he completely dwarfed the serving counter and the ladle he was holding looked more like a teaspoon in his vast hand.

Phibs reached out to stop Paddington. "Mate," he said, his forehead creased in concern, "I really wouldn't."

Paddington smiled, however, and patted Phibs's hand. 'Don't worry. Aunt Lucy said if you look for the good in people you'll always find it."

Spoon shook his head and muttered, "She's obviously

never met Knuckles."

Every single prisoner went quiet as Paddington made his way over to the chef. Their cutlery stopped halfway to their mouths. They put their knives and forks down and sat, as quiet as mice, waiting to see what would happen next.

Paddington went up to the counter and rapped on it with his paw to get the man's attention. "Excuse me, Mr. Knuckles?" he said.

The man turned slowly and Paddington took in a sharp breath to steady himself as he came face-to-face with him.

"Yes . . . ?" growled the chef, his face twisted into an angry expression.

Not one prisoner dared move a muscle. Every one of them was holding his breath.

The warden brought his radio to his mouth and whispered nervously into it. "Send a medic to the canteen," he said. "Quick!"

Paddington gulped as he saw the look on the huge chef's face. "I just wondered if I could have a quick word about the food?" he asked in a small voice.

"You want to complain?" Knuckles asked, smiling slowly.

Paddington shook his head. "Oh, no, no! I wouldn't say that."

"That's a shame," said Knuckles. His smile widened, but it didn't reach his eyes. "I love it when people complain," he said. His huge fist circled a rolling pin, gripping it tightly.

"Oh really?" said Paddington. He relaxed. "In that case, I think you should know that the food is unfortunately rather gritty AND lumpy, and as for the bread . . ." He picked up a baguette and hit it against Knuckle's head, knocking his cap askew. "Need I say more?" Paddington continued, oblivious to the mounting tension in the room behind him—and Knuckles's tightening grip on the rolling pin. "I think we need to completely overhaul the menu," Paddington went on, warming to his theme. "Now I know we're working to a tight budget, but I think we could at least add some sauce."

Paddington picked up a bottle of ketchup and accidently squirted some on to the chef's apron.

"Oops, sorry about." Paddington grabbed a cloth and tried to wipe off the sauce, but a stain was quickly spreading. "Never mind, I know how to get rid of that," he went on, picking up a bottle of mustard.

He squirted it on top of the ketchup, but then had second thoughts. "Hang on—maybe it's not mustard?" he pondered. Then, turning to the rest of the room, he asked the other men, "Does anyone know what gets rid of ketchup stains?"

But not a prisoner was to be seen—they were all hiding under the tables!

Paddington looked puzzled, while the warden whispered frantically into his radio, "Forget the medic—better call for a priest."

Paddington turned back to Knuckles.

The chef growled, leaned forward, and snapped the rolling pin in two!

Paddington realized his mistake. "I'm s-sorry, Mr. Knuckles, sir—" he began, cowering.

The chef leaned right over the counter and lifted Paddington into the air. "Now listen to me, you little maggot," he snarled.

"Listening," Paddington croaked.

"Nobody criticizes my food," said Knuckles.

"Right," said Paddington, nodding enthusiastically.

"Nobody squirts condiments on my apron," Knuckles continued.

"Got it," rasped Paddington.

"Nobody bonks me on the head with a baguette."

"No bonking." Paddington nodded again.

"I'll overhaul the menu all right," said Knuckles through gritted teeth.

"W-will you?" Paddington stammered.

"And you know what the dish of the day will be . . . ? Bear pie!" the chef finished with a roar.

Paddington gasped, and without thinking, he reached quickly under his hat and whipped out a marmalade sandwich that he had managed to hide from the warden since his arrival. He squashed it straight into the chef's mouth.

Then he closed his eyes and waited for the end . . .

The whole room waited with him.

No one dared move.

There was a chewing sound, followed by a gulping and a swallowing noise and then Paddington heard Knuckles growl, "What *was* that?"

Paddington opened one eye. "A marmalade sandwich," he said.

"Marmalade?" Knuckles repeated, his expression softening.

"My Aunt Lucy taught me how to make it," Paddington said, opening his other eye. He reasoned that perhaps if he could keep the man talking, he could save himself.

Knuckles slowly lowered Paddington on to the counter. "You mean you can make more of these?" he asked, his eyes glinting.

A murmur ran through the canteen as the prisoners

wondered what was going to happen next.

"I can," said Paddington. The thought of his Aunt Lucy had made him feel suddenly much braver.

Knuckles turned his attention to the rest of the room. "Get off the floor, you bunch of yellow-bellies, and listen up!" he roared to the prisoners. "This bear is now under my protection. Anyone who touches a hair on his back will answer to me—Knuckles McGinty. That's Knuckles with a capital 'N,' all right?" he snarled.

"Thank you, Mr. McGinty," Paddington gasped.

"Don't thank me yet. I don't do nuthin' for no one for nuthin'," Knuckles replied. "You get my protection so long as you make me that marmalade. Deal?" Knuckles spat on his hand and offered it to Paddington, who, looking puzzled, spat on it too before saying, "Deal!"

Knuckles glared at Paddington, then throwing back his head he bellowed with laughter. "You're a funny one and no mistake! Now . . . let's get to work!"

CHAPTER 11
Madame Kozlova Tells Her Story

Mrs. Brown told the family about her conversation with Mr. Gruber.

"If there's one person who can tell us more about the pop-up book, it is Madame Kozlova herself," she said. "I'm going to go and see her to ask her what she knows."

Mr. Brown wasn't sure it was such a good idea, but even he had to admit that they couldn't sit around doing nothing while poor Paddington was in prison. "All right," he said. "But I'm coming with you," he said, grabbing his coat.

"And me!" said Judy.

"Me too!" said Jonathan.

The glamorous fortune-teller was not exactly pleased to see them. She observed them with a tight-lipped expression.

"Ah, so you're the family whose bear stole my pop-up book?" she said.

"No, no!" Judy cried. "That's why we're here. We think the real thief broke into Mr. Gruber's shop to steal the book and Paddington disturbed him."

"Paddington wouldn't do such a thing," Mrs. Brown assured Madame Kozlova. "That's why we wanted to talk to you. Is there anything you could tell us about the pop-up book? Anything that could be useful to help us track down the thief?"

Madame Kozlova could see that the family really believed that Paddington was innocent. She was not an unkind woman, so she relented.

"All right," she said with a smile. "Let's see, now . . . my great-grandmother who started this fair made the pop-up book," Madame Kozlova said in her heavy Russian accent. "She made lots of them— to remember *every single* city she visited." She paused. "But you may be right that there is something that would interest a thief about this one—there is quite a particular story behind it," she said.

"Go on," said Mr. Brown, leaning forward.

"My great-grandmother was quite a show-woman," said Madame Kozlova with a smile. "She could tame lions, you know. And breathe fire and swallow swords. However, she was most famous for the trapeze. They called her the Flying Swan. Imagine," she said, waving her arm in a dramatic gesture. "It is the 1930s . . . Wherever my great-grandmother went she was showered with gifts . . ."

The Browns sat back, picturing what the glamorous fortune-teller was describing.

"She was every man's favorite. Over the years, she made a fortune from all the presents she was given. One man even gave her a necklace of *real diamonds*," Madame Kozlova said, her eyes shining.

"How romantic," breathed Mrs. Brown.

"Ah, but where there is fortune there is also jealousy," said Madame Kozlova, grimacing. "There was a magician who worked for the fair who was a brilliant but envious man. He wanted my great-grandmother's fortune for himself!"

"Oh no," whispered Mrs. Brown. She was completely caught up in the story. "What did he do?"

"Something terrible," said Madame Kozlova, lowering her voice. "One day, he cut through the trapeze rope." She made a scissors motion with her hand. "The Flying Swan became the Dying Swan . . ."

Mrs. Brown gasped. "No!"

"Yes," said the fortune-teller. "My great-grandmother plummeted to the floor. The magician was the first on the scene. He rushed over, pretending to be concerned. But while he was checking my great-grand-mother for signs of life, he took a key chain from round her neck. Then he slipped away into the crowd before anyone could stop him."

Mr. and Mrs. Brown exchanged glances.

"He went straight to my great-grandmother's cara-van," the fortune-teller continued, "and he opened up her safe, but instead of her treasure all he found inside was her pop-up book of London."

"Serves him right," said Mrs. Brown grimly.

Madame Kozlova nodded. "Quite so," she said. "The police came after him," she went on, "but he disap-peared in a puff of smoke, leaving only the book behind. To this day no one knows where my great-grandmoth-er's fortune is hidden."

"That is a tragic story," said Mrs. Brown, dabbing at her eyes.

"Yes, and it doesn't get us any closer to understanding what on earth the thief wants with the book," said Mr. Brown grimly. "Thank you, Madame Kozlova. You have been most generous with your time."

The family headed back to 32 Windsor Gardens, their hearts heavy as they wondered what they could do now to prove Paddington's innocence.

Later that evening, Mrs. Brown was sitting up in bed, drawing a picture of Madame Kozlova. "There's got to be something we're missing," she said thoughtfully.

Mr. Brown called out from the bathroom. "So you keep saying, but what exactly? The stuff about the Flying Swan was a good yarn, but as for the book . . . Madame Kozlova told us—it's just a homemade pop-up book."

"I know," said Mrs. Brown. "But have you thought about why it was kept in a safe?"

Mr. Brown came out of the bathroom wearing a blue face mask. "You're not telling me you believe all that guff she told us about the magician?" he said scornfully.

Mrs. Brown ignored him. "She put twelve London landmarks in that book," she said. "What if they are clues?"

"Clues?" Mr. Brown pulled a face. "Clues to what?"

"To where the great-grandmother had hidden her fortune!" Mrs. Brown said.

"You mean, like a treasure map?" Mr. Brown said. He was still skeptical.

"Exactly," said Mrs. Brown. She sat up excitedly. "That would explain why the thief took it from Mr. Gruber's."

Mr. Brown began wiping off his face mask. "I keep telling you—that fortune-teller spun you a yarn. It's what they do," he said.

Mrs. Brown looked annoyed suddenly. "Honestly, darling, you're so close-minded these days."

Mr. Brown bristled. "What's that supposed to mean?"

"What happened to Bull's-eye Brown?" Mrs. Brown retorted. "The man who sent coconuts flying with one hurl of a ball? He'd have believed me."

Mr. Brown picked up a hand mirror and checked the wrinkles around his eyes. "He's gone, Mary," he said, turning back to his wife. "You're married to a creaky old man, not Bull's-eye Brown."

Mrs. Brown tutted.

Mr. Brown ignored her. "The point is, we're not going to help Paddington by going on a wild-goose chase. We're looking for this scruffy chancer," he said, pointing to the picture on the poster Mrs. Brown and Judy had made, "not some swashbuckling pirate who's hunting for treasure."

"Well, I think there's more to him than meets the eye," Mrs. Brown huffed. "I think he somehow knew the story of the Kozlova fortune and is out there now, trying to find it."

Mr. Brown shrugged. "It can't be the same man as in Madame Kozlova's story—that magician would be about one hundred and fifty by now. Remember she said everything happened in the 1930s."

"We should be out there this minute, trying to catch him in the act, Henry!" Mrs. Brown protested.

Mr. Brown snorted. "Not right now, we're not," he said, getting into bed next to his wife. "I'm going to get some beauty sleep. Goodness knows I need it." And with that, he turned out the light and put an end to the conversation.

Meanwhile, as the Browns slept, a procession of nuns was slowly climbing the steps of St. Paul's Cathedral. It was a dark, moonless and silent night. The black of the nuns' habits gave them a mysterious air as they walked softly along, merging with the shadows of the cold stone walls of the cathedral. It would not be difficult for one of them to slip away unnoticed . . .

Phoenix Buchanan knew this, which is why he had come to find his next clue dressed as one of the nuns! He waited until he was sure no one could see him, and then he sneaked out of the procession and ran up a staircase to the Whispering Gallery.

"Grandfather," he said to himself, "I am doing this in your memory. They never appreciated your full worth as a magician. Why should all the money and jewels have gone to that ridiculous Flying Swan woman? Her act was no better than yours, I'm sure. People just don't recognize true artistic talent when they see it. And I should know . . ."

He sighed dramatically and made a beeline for an angel statue that he had seen in the pop-up book. Then he swiftly ducked down to look at the bottom of the statue, where he had spotted a letter, much like the one on Tower Bridge. It was carved into the marble base.

"'A,'" he whispered, making a note. "Two down, ten more to go—"

"Oi! What d'you think you're doing?"

Phoenix jumped up, startled by a security guard who was waving at him and shouting into a walkie-talkie at the same time.

"ATTENTION, ALL UNITS!" he yelled.

Phoenix panicked and caught the edge of the statue with his elbow. It teetered, and then toppled over, smashing into pieces.

"AN UNUSUALLY ATTRACTIVE NUN IS CAUSING MAYHEM IN THE CATHEDRAL DOME!" the guard shouted as Phoenix ran, shedding his nun's habit as he went. "CLOSE IN! CLOSE IN!" the guard bellowed.

Phoenix was too quick, however. By the time he had arrived at the bottom of the steps, he had changed his disguise and was wearing an archbishop's robes. He passed the guards quietly without attracting a second glance and disappeared into the night . . .

CHAPTER 12
Aunt Lucy's Recipe Saves the Day

The next morning the prison warden dragged a very sleepy Paddington out of bed and down the corridors to the canteen where Knuckles was waiting for him to report for marmalade duty.

"Mr. McGinty?" Paddington said once the warden had left.

"What do you want?" Knuckles growled.

"Well, the thing is," Paddington began, "I'm actually innocent—and I wondered if you had any advice on how to clear my name? Now that we're friends . . ." He tailed off as he took in the look of amusement on Knuckles's face.

"Friends?" Knuckles exclaimed. "I'm your boss, not your buddy."

"In that case, after you," said Paddington, holding the door open.

"Why?" said Knuckles, looking suspicious. "So you can stab me in the back?"

"No!" Paddington protested. "Because it's polite. Aunt

Lucy said if you're kind and polite the world will be right."

Knuckles snorted. "You were in front of me and now you're behind—that makes you a sap."

Paddington didn't know what to make of this comment so he decided it was best not to comment. He followed Knuckles into the kitchen. "Where's everyone else?" he asked, looking around the empty room.

"I work alone," said Knuckles. "'Trust no one and expect the worst,' that's my philosophy." He grunted. "Ingredients are over there," he went on, pointing to the cupboards. "Get on with it then!" he said, as Paddington hesitated.

"Aren't you going to help, Mr. Knuckles?" he asked.

"No!" Knuckles exclaimed, flopping into a chair.

"But I can't do this on my own," Paddington protested. "There are five hundred hungry prisoners wanting breakfast! I'm going to need to squeeze one thousand juicy oranges."

Knuckles opened a copy of the *Hard Times* and said, "Rule number one—no talking."

Paddington nodded. He took an apron and began humming instead.

"Rule number two—no humming, no singing, and no expressions of bonhomie," growled Knuckles.

Paddington stopped humming. He reached up to the top shelf and pulled at a heavy sack of oranges. It didn't budge.

He tried again, straining and heaving. Still it wouldn't move. He looked at Knuckles, who was still reading his paper.

Paddington gave one last tug at the sack. It moved a little way, but there was a worrying rumbling sound as the other sacks shifted as well. Paddington gasped and moved back, but he wasn't fast enough. Every single one of the sacks came crashing down, falling on top of Paddington and covering him completely.

"Ow!" he said in a muffled voice.

Knuckles gave a heavy sigh, and then, rising to his feet, he came and took the sacks off.

"I'm finding this working environment extremely stressful," said Paddington, brushing himself down. "Aunt Lucy says that—"

"AUNT LUCY!" Knuckles roared. "I've had it up to here with Aunt Lucy." He threw his enormous hands in the air. "She sounds like a proper old bag to me."

Paddington looked up at Knuckles and said carefully, "I beg your pardon?"

Knuckles took a deep breath and glared at Paddington. "Aunt Lucy sounds like the most naive, mushy-brained, gullible . . ." He paused.

Paddington's face had taken on rather a strange expression.

"What're you doing? What's going on?" Knuckles

asked with a puzzled frown.

Paddington had locked eyes with the chef and was giving him a very firm look.

Knuckles began to feel uncomfortable. He broke out in a cold sweat and pulled at his collar awkwardly. "It's suddenly got very hot in here. Did I leave the oven on?"

"No," said Paddington. "I'm giving you a Hard Stare. Aunt Lucy taught me how to do them when people have forgotten their manners."

"Phew. Pretty impressive for a bear, I'll give you that," said Knuckles, shifting uneasily under Paddington's gaze.

"Now, Mr. McGinty, I may look like a hardened criminal to you," said Paddington, relaxing his stare a little, "but the fact is I'm innocent. My family is working hard to clear my name so if you want me to make you some marmalade before I leave this place, you'd better give me a hand. I can't do it all on my own. Everything takes longer with paws," he added in explanation.

"All right, I'll help," said Knuckles. The hard stare had clearly worked. "I doubt I'll be much use to you, though." He held up his huge fists. "These weren't exactly made for cooking either."

"Oh, I don't know," said Paddington. "They look like a great pair of orange squeezers to me."

"Orange squeezers?"

Paddington handed Knuckles an orange and a bowl. "Have a go," he said.

The huge man took the orange and crushed it in one go. Juice poured out into the bowl.

Paddington beamed. "We'll soon have this lot done," he said.

They got into a rhythm then, with Paddington sniffing out the ripest oranges and Knuckles squeezing them into a pan.

"You have to be careful with knives, Aunt Lucy says," said Paddington.

Knuckles took a knife and chopped the rind into pieces with the speed of machine-gun fire.

"Where did you learn how to do that?" Paddington asked, his eyes wide in wonder.

"Trust me. You don't want to know," said Knuckles with a sly grin.

Soon the oranges were ready. Paddington added spices and lemon and lots and lots of sugar.

Knuckles leaned in and sniffed. "Well?" he asked Paddington. "Is it any good?"

"We'll only know when it's set," said Paddington, settling down to wait. He hoped it would be perfect. He didn't like to think what Knuckles might have to say to him otherwise.

CHAPTER 13

Read All About It!

Judy had managed to print a pile of newspapers at school featuring her article and some of her mother's sketches of the thief. She was determined that people should read the truth about Paddington because all the other papers were spreading lies about him.

"I'm going to take them to the kiosk," she told her parents one morning. "Miss Kitts might be able to sell them for me."

"I'll come with you," said Jonathan.

They arrived at the kiosk to find the Colonel having a cup of coffee with Miss Kitts.

Judy showed them her newspapers. The headline read "NEW THEORY EMERGES IN PADDINGTON CASE."

"Would you mind selling these for me, Miss Kitts?" Judy asked. "I thought I'd write my own report on the case," she explained.

"Did you do this yourself?" the Colonel asked. He

took a copy and flicked through it, impressed.

"Jonathan gave me a hand," Judy replied.

Jonathan was about to agree when he caught sight of a group of boys in shades approaching the kiosk. He pulled his own shades down and said to his sister, "It's J-Dog, okay? And don't tell anyone about the paper—not cool."

Judy rolled her eyes.

Miss Kitts smiled. "I'll do my best to shift them, darling," she said, "but we've got a lot of competition this morning." She gestured to the other papers, which all had the news of the strange goings-on at St. Paul's the night before.

"Terrible business at the cathedral," said the Colonel.

Judy read the story. "This is weird," she said.

Miss Kitts agreed. "'Specially after the shenanigans at Tower Bridge."

Jonathan forgot about being cool for a second. "Wow," he said. "Aren't they two of the places in the pop-up book?"

"Maybe Mum IS on to something—maybe the book does have clues in it!" Judy said. "Come on, let's go and tell her."

And they ran back to 32 Windsor Gardens, chattering excitedly.

As soon as they arrived back home, Judy and Jonathan explained their theory to their mother.

"I think you're right," said Mrs. Brown, "the goings-on at Tower Bridge and the cathedral have to be linked!"

"But what can we do, Mum?" Judy asked.

"There's only one thing *to* do," said Mrs. Brown. "We'll have to go to St. Paul's right away to see if we can find any evidence. Come on!" she said, grabbing her coat.

The three of them arrived at the cathedral just as a group was setting off on a tour of the building. A guide was talking, so Mrs. Brown, Judy, and Jonathan slotted in behind the group and listened in.

"Designed by Sir Christopher Wren, St. Paul's is one of London's most famous landmarks," the guide was saying. "Follow me to the Whispering Gallery . . ."

They went up the stairs into the circular room.

"Around the Whispering Gallery there are eight—" The guide paused. The area was closed off with police tape. "Oh," he said, counting the angels. "Sorry, *seven* priceless angels," he corrected himself.

Judy broke away from the tour group and went up to a guard. "Excuse me," she asked, "what happened here?"

"A nun went berserk—it happens," the guard said airily. He nodded to a chapel where one hundred nuns were being held. One elderly nun came out with a walker.

The guard saw her and called out, "Hold it, Sister!" He held up his hand. "No one leaves until the detective says they can."

The old nun made a face and went back into the chapel.

The guard turned back to Judy. "The police have rounded them all up, but if you ask me the culprit has already slipped the net."

Jonathan and Mrs. Brown had joined Judy. "What makes you say that?" Jonathan asked.

"Because I saw her, that's what," said the guard. His expression became dreamy. "And she had the face of an angel," he added with a sigh.

Mrs. Brown took a pencil out of her hair. "Can you describe her?" she asked, getting ready to sketch.

The guard gave a silly grin. "With pleasure," he said.

CHAPTER 14

Marmalade Is Served

Back in the prison, Paddington and Knuckles were getting ready to serve breakfast to a canteen full of hungry men.

"Good morning, gentlemen," said Paddington, addressing the room. "Chef McGinty would like to propose for your delight an orange marmalade served on a warm crustless slice of bread, topped with another slice of crustless bread. *Bon appétit.*"

The prisoners did not move. They sat in silence, staring at their plates.

Knuckles stuck his head through the hatch and yelled, "Take it or leave it!" before disappearing from view, slamming the hatch shut behind him.

Paddington stared after the chef as the men began muttering to one another.

"Please excuse me," Paddington said to the prisoners. He went into the kitchen to find Knuckles sulking.

"Why don't you come and join the others?" Paddington said in an encouraging tone.

"Don't want to," Knuckles mumbled.

"Why not? Are you scared what they might think?" Paddington asked.

"NO!" Knuckles shouted. His expression then immediately crumpled and he asked anxiously, "What *do* they think? Did they like it? What did they say?"

"Well—" Paddington began.

Knuckles didn't give him a chance to finish. He flew into a tantrum, kicking over pans and knocking over tins and packets. "I knew it!" he yelled. "They hate it, don't they? My father always said I would amount to nuthin' and he was right!"

Paddington peeped out of the hatch and put a paw out to calm the chef down. "Knuckles, Knuckles!"

"WHAT?"

"Come and look!" said Paddington, gesturing through the hatch to what was going on in the canteen.

Knuckles came over to join Paddington. He looked out to see every single one of the prisoners devouring their sandwiches. They were making ecstatic noises, smiling, licking their lips and groaning with delight. The marmalade sandwiches were clearly the most delicious food the men had tasted in years.

Paddington lives with the Browns and Mrs. Bird in London. He loves his new home.

Mrs. Brown is training to swim across the English Channel to France.

Mr. Brown is practicing chakrabatics.

Judy Brown is starting her own newspaper.

Jonathan Brown is trying to be cool but secretly loves steam trains.

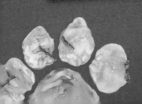

Everyone is excited about Madame Kozlova's Steam Fair! The actor Phoenix Buchanan is opening the show.

Paddington wants to buy a special gift for Aunt Lucy's one hundredth birthday. Mr. Gruber is letting him look through Madame Kozlova's old trunk and Paddington has found a beautiful rare pop-up book. It shows London's magnificent landmarks.

Paddington decides he will earn the money
for Aunt Lucy's gift by washing windows.

"Come on." Paddington held out his paw. "You need to let them thank you." Paddington led a reluctant Knuckles into the room. The prisoners immediately leaped to their feet and gave the chef a raucous standing ovation, cheering and clapping and stamping. "Three cheers for Knuckles!" one of them cried. "Hip hip hooray! Hip hip hooray! Hip hip hooray!"

Everyone joined in.

Knuckles glowed with pride and happiness.

Phibs, the Australian, called out, "Great tucker, mate. You got anything else? For pudding?"

Knuckles's face began to rearrange itself into its usual expression of anger.

Paddington saw it and, thinking on his paws, he stepped in quickly to prevent another explosion. "We only know how to make marmalade, I'm afraid. Unless you know any recipes . . . ?"

"This lot doesn't know their paprika from their pectin, Paddington," Knuckles snarled.

Spoon piped up, "My great-grandmother used to make a lovely chocolate roulade. I think I can remember the recipe."

"Charley Rumble makes a mean apple crumble," said another prisoner.

"I can do strawberry *panna cotta* with a pomegranate

glaze," offered T-Bone.

Paddington beamed. "That sounds wonderful, doesn't it, Knuckles?"

Knuckles was beaming too. "Yeah!" he said. "Let's get cooking!"

Over the next month, Paddington got to work on the prison menu. Afternoon tea quickly became an institution. Every day at four o'clock, Paddington would walk the length of the canteen with a dessert trolley groaning with piles of delicious cakes. The canteen itself was transformed into a delightful tearoom with gingham tablecloths.

"This is the life," said T-Bone one afternoon. He was tucking into a giant slice of Victoria sponge filled to bursting with raspberry jam and whipped cream.

"Why didn't we think of this before?" said Spoon. He licked his lips and took a bite of a gooey Bakewell tart.

"It's the perfect way to spend the afternoon," said another prisoner called the Professor. He picked up a piece of cake.

"Ahem," said Paddington, passing by with the trolley. "Excuse me, Professor, but what would Aunt Lucy say?" he asked, eyeing the Professor's fingers.

The Professor looked sheepish. "Always use a cake fork," he said meekly.

"Well then!" said Paddington.

The Professor put the cake down, then, using the fork, he shoveled the whole slice into his mouth in one go.

Paddington tutted. "It is going to take a while for you all to learn your manners," he said.

But learn them they did—over time the prisoners became very skilled at using cake forks, tucking napkins into the front of their uniforms and remembering to say "please" and "thank you."

The warden was so delighted with the prisoners' behavior—and so full of cake himself—that even he slowly became more relaxed. In fact, it was not long before he was reading stories at bedtime through the loudspeakers.

Everyone was happy.

Except Paddington.

The night before visiting day he sat in his cell and looked at the photo he had of himself with the Browns and Mrs. Bird.

"I can't wait to see you all," he said with a sigh. He stared longingly at the picture of the family he missed so much. "It's all very well having new friends and a lot of delicious food, but this place isn't home. I only hope you will be bringing me good news."

The Browns did bring news—but it was not good news. They showed Paddington a newspaper with pictures of a nun, a beefeater, and a king. The pictures were accompanied by the words: "Three shadowy figures spotted snooping around London landmarks this week." There was also another image of Paddington with a story underneath that told how he had broken into Mr. Gruber's and was now getting his "just desserts."

"Well, the last part is true," said Paddington. He wiped the remnants of some cream from his whiskers. "At least the food is good here now."

"Don't worry, Paddington," said Judy. She spoke through a microphone on the other side of a glass partition. "We'll get you out of here. We think we've made a breakthrough—it looks as though the thief you saw is part of a criminal gang."

"And they're using the pop-up book as a treasure map!" Jonathan added.

Mr. Brown was the only member of the family who seemed unconvinced. "Well, it's a theory," he said begrudgingly.

"Do you know who they are?" Paddington said,

looking through the glass at the pictures.

"Not yet, dearie," said Mrs. Bird.

Knuckles appeared suddenly behind Paddington. "Maybe I should take a look," he said, leaning over the bear's shoulder.

Mr. Brown bristled. "Excuse me," he said. "This is a private conversation."

"It's all right, Mr. Brown," said Paddington. He turned and smiled up at the chef. "This is my friend Knuckles."

Knuckles grinned. "How do you do?" he asked the Browns.

Immediately a host of other faces appeared with Knuckles.

Paddington began a long introduction. "This is Phibs . . . Spoon . . ." He pointed to each prisoner in turn. "Jimmy the Snitch . . . T-Bone . . . the Professor . . . Squeaky Pete . . ."

"Hello!" said Squeaky Pete in a high-pitched voice.

"Double Bass Bob . . ."

"Hello," said Double Bass Bob in a very deep voice.

"This is Farmer Jack," Paddington went on. "Old-timer . . . Mad Dog . . . Sir Geoffrey Willcot . . ."

"I hope I can rely on your vote?" said Sir Geoffrey.

"Johnny Cashpoint," said Paddington.

"Kerching!" said Johnny.

"And Charley Rumble."

Charley growled and Mr. Brown jumped in alarm.

Mrs. Brown was charmed. "It's so lovely to meet you all," she said with a warm smile. "I must say it is such a relief to know that Paddington has already made such sweet friends."

"Would you excuse me for a moment?" Mr. Brown said to Paddington. He leaned over and flicked a switch on the countertop. The lights went out on the Browns' side of the glass. "What are you DOING, Mary?" he said.

"I'm talking to the nice men," his wife replied.

Mrs. Bird smirked.

"NICE MEN?" Mr. Brown exclaimed. "We can't trust this lot. I mean, look at them! Talk about a rogues' gallery. Hideous. As for that bearded baboon in the middle—he hasn't got two brain cells to rub together—"

"We can still hear you, Mr. Brown." Knuckles's voice came through the microphone.

Mr. Brown froze.

"That was the light you turned off, Mr. Brown," Knuckles went on. "The microphone switch is the one that says 'microphone' on it."

Judy rolled her eyes and flicked the light back on.

Mr. Brown swallowed nervously. "Gentlemen, if I have offended you in any way—" he began.

Knuckles grinned. "Don't worry about it," he said. "We're fond of the little fella." He ruffled Paddington's fur. "About the pictures in that paper, though," he said, pointing to the photos. "You should realize that if anyone can recognize a criminal gang it's us lot."

Judy sat up and said eagerly. "Really?" she said. "That's amazing. We'd be so grateful for your help." She held the paper up to the glass again. "Recognize any of them?"

Knuckles took a good look, then shaking his head, he said, "'Fraid not—lads?"

All the prisoners shook their heads.

Sir Geoffrey said primly, "I'm afraid I couldn't possibly comment."

"I'm sorry to say it," Knuckles said to Paddington, "but I think your family are barking up the wrong tree. A nun, a beefeater, and a king? Looks more like a fancy-dress party than a criminal gang to me."

Poor Paddington was completely crestfallen. "What are we going to do now?" he asked.

The Browns looked at one another sadly.

Mrs. Bird leaned forward and looked Paddington in the eye. "Don't despair, dearie," she said firmly. "We'll have you out of here soon. You must just sit tight for now."

It doesn't look as though I have much choice, thought Paddington.

CHAPTER 15

Phoenix Buchanan Acts the Innocent

Autumn turned into winter and the Browns missed Paddington more than ever. They were still trying everything they could to get his name cleared. Judy had printed yet another edition of her newspaper and Mrs. Brown was on her way to deliver them to Miss Kitts. She left 32 Windsor Gardens, thinking sadly of poor Paddington locked in his cell. She walked past all the friends that Paddington used to greet on his daily trips to see Mr. Gruber. Everyone was trying to get on with their lives as normal, but some were finding this harder than others—Dr. Jafri, for one.

"Bottoms!" he exclaimed as he locked himself out of his house again. Then, catching sight of Mrs. Brown, he blushed and said, "Ah, sorry."

Mrs. Brown smiled sadly. "That's all right," she said.

"Windsor Gardens just isn't the same without Paddington, is it?" said Dr. Jafri.

Mrs. Brown shook her head, sighing, and went on her way to the newspaper kiosk.

As she walked down the street she passed Mr. Curry, who was berating Fred Barnes, the garbage collector. He was sitting on the back of his parked truck, reading an A–Z map of London.

"You can't park here!" Mr. Curry barked.

"I'm not parked," said Fred. "I'm doing the bins."

"You are not!" Mr. Curry exclaimed. "You're studying—I know your game. You're studying to be a black cab driver, aren't you?" he said, gesturing to the map of London. "And on council time too. I could report you for this."

Mrs. Brown rolled her eyes as she passed him. She walked over to the kiosk and saw that the Colonel was there talking to Miss Kitts.

"Morning, Colonel! Morning, Miss Kitts!" she called. She handed a bundle of Judy's newspapers to Miss Kitts. "Judy asked me to drop these off," she said.

Mr. Curry came over and picked up one of the newspapers.

"Uh-oh," the Colonel muttered. "Here comes trouble."

"What's this?" said Mr. Curry, scouring the front page of the newspaper. "Propaganda! You're wasting your time trying to peddle that rubbish," he snarled at Mrs. Brown. "Everyone knows your bear did it. And this street is a better place without him." He was distracted from saying more when he spotted Wolfie, the stray dog that had helped Paddington chase the thief. "Oi!" he shouted at the dog. "Get out of here, you mangy hound! You should be taken to the dog pound." And he ran off after Wolfie.

Mrs. Brown exchanged knowing looks with Miss Kitts and the Colonel.

"He doesn't change, does he?" said the Colonel.

"Give them here, Mary," said Miss Kitts. "I have to sell them under the counter, but people are buying them, you know."

"Really?" said Mrs. Brown. She was heartened at the news.

Miss Kitts nodded. "More than you might think," she said.

"It's a bloomin' good read," said the Colonel. "Made a couple of people think twice about your young bear," he added. He smiled kindly.

"You just need to find that thief," said Miss Kitts, patting Mrs. Brown on the arm.

"We're trying," said Mrs. Brown with a sigh. She turned to Miss Kitts's parrot, who was sitting on a pile of newspapers nibbling at his claw. "I don't suppose you know where the thief is, do you, Feathers?"

The parrot looked at her with his beady eye. "He's behind you!" he squawked.

"I'm sorry?" said Mrs. Brown, frowning.

"Mary!" said a familiar voice.

Mrs. Brown turned to see Phoenix Buchanan waving from his balcony.

"Oh, hello, Phoenix!" Mrs. Brown called back.

"Come on in, I want to hear all about the investigation," Phoenix said, waving her over to his house.

Mrs. Brown was intrigued. She said goodbye to Miss Kitts and the Colonel and went over the road to where Phoenix was now waiting at his front door.

The actor invited Mrs. Brown into his living room. It was a huge room, lavishly decorated with throws, rugs, and paintings. Mrs. Brown couldn't help noticing a particularly enormous portrait of Phoenix himself posing on a rock in the Scottish Highlands, wearing a kilt. She edged away from it and sat down.

"Come on, then, Mrs. Brown," Phoenix said, his eyes shining. "Tell me all the news."

"It's hard to know where to start," said Mrs. Brown. "Some very mysterious things have been happening."

"What sort of things?" asked Phoenix.

"Well, strange people have been spotted at every

landmark in that pop-up book that the thief stole from Mr. Gruber's," Mrs. Brown said. "*Very* strange people—in sort of fancy-dress costumes."

"*Really?*" said Phoenix with exaggerated interest.

Mrs. Brown shook her head. "Perhaps it's all a coincidence. Henry says I've let my imagination run away with me."

"Well, you're an *artist*, Mrs. Brown, like me," said Phoenix indulgently. "We let our imaginations run free, don't we? It's what makes us special." He paused and put on a more serious expression. "Have to say, though, I fear old Henry might be right about this one."

Mrs. Brown looked at him despondently. "Great. That means we are back to square one."

"Listen," said Phoenix. He sat up and leaned forward as though about to deliver some very important information. "I've got something to tell you that might turn that little frown upside down. It looks like the funding is coming through for my one-man show!" He paused to let his exciting news sink in.

It did not have the desired effect.

"Oh, right," Mrs. Brown said, visibly unimpressed.

Phoenix tried harder to pique Mrs. Brown's interest. "It'll be an evening of monologues and song—all my greatest creations back on the stage. I call it *The Phoenix*

Rises! Of course, you and your family will get free tickets to the opening night. But how about I give you a little preview right now? This one's from *Follies*." Phoenix struck a pose and counted himself in to a song. "A-one, two, three, four . . . 'Listen to the rain on the roof go pit-pitty-pat' . . ."

Mrs. Brown was not really paying attention, however, and her frown had certainly not turned "upside down."

Phoenix stopped and looked mildly offended. "What's the matter? Don't you like musicals?"

"It's not that," said Mrs. Brown sadly. "It just seems strange that Paddington's still in prison and yet life still carries on."

Phoenix's face collapsed into a fake expression of sympathy and regret. "Oh, I *know*," he said. "It must be hard to accept that he's won—the man with the dazzling blue eyes."

Mrs. Brown snapped to attention. "What did you say?"

Phoenix saw his mistake and began to babble. "I mean . . . the man on your poster—in your wonderful drawing. His eyes are startling, don't you think?" he said.

"But how did you know he had blue eyes?" said Mrs. Brown. "It's a pencil sketch." She rummaged in her bag and brought out a poster.

"Oh, so it is," said Phoenix. He made an effort to recover his composure. "Well, it must have been the way you capture the light," he said casually. "It obviously made me *think* he had blue eyes. You're *such* a good artist."

But Mrs. Brown was not listening to Phoenix's empty flattery. She was thinking of all the sketches she had done since Paddington had gone to prison. She stared at Phoenix Buchanan now as though she was seeing him in a completely new light.

Back at home in the Browns' kitchen, Mrs. Brown explained her theory to the rest of the family. They listened intently as she told them how Phoenix had reacted.

Mr. Brown was not convinced by his wife's idea.

"Phoenix Buchanan?" he exclaimed. "You really are letting your imagination run away with you now, Mary."

"You have to admit, as an actor, he *is* a master of disguise," Mrs. Brown persisted.

"She's gone mad," Mr. Brown muttered to the others.

Mrs. Brown was not going to be put off that easily, however. "Think about it, Henry. Somewhere out there is the missing treasure—"

"Alleged fortune," Mr. Brown corrected her.

"And Knuckles said we weren't looking for a criminal

gang," Mrs. Brown reminded him.

Judy had picked up on her mother's train of thought. "Because there *was* no gang!" she cried.

Jonathan was following too. "It was *one man*!" he said.

Mrs. Brown nodded. Her eyes shone with excitement. "And Feathers knew all along," she said.

"Feathers?" asked Henry. "Who's Feathers?"

"No one," said Mrs. Brown quickly, realizing she may have gone too far.

But it was too late, Mr. Brown had worked out what she meant. "The parrot at the newsstand?" he said in disbelief. "You're not going to take seriously the testimony of a talking bird now, are you?"

Mrs. Brown stared at her hands and said nothing.

Mr. Brown let out an exasperated noise. "Can we please return to planet Earth for one minute?" he said. "Phoenix Buchanan is a highly respected and award-winning actor, not to mention a member of my company's Platinum Club. He is *not* a petty thief. And before you go casting aspersions about a pillar of our community, Mary, I might remind you that you don't have any proof." He glared at his wife, then, getting up from the table, walked out of the room, saying, "If anyone wants me, I shall be at the law library." And with that he slammed the door behind him.

"He's right," said Judy. "We do need proof."

Mrs. Bird patted Mrs. Brown's hand. "Well, I believe you, Mary," she said. "Actors are some of the most evil, devious people on the planet. They lie for a living. If we're going to catch one, we'll need a foolproof plan."

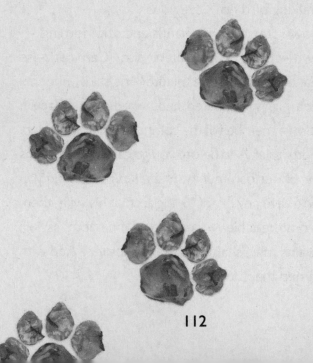

CHAPTER 16

The Browns Have a Master Plan

Over in Portobello Prison, Paddington's new friends were coming up with a plan of their own.

Paddington was fast asleep in his cell when he was awoken by a loud metallic *CLANG*.

He sat up and blinked. "What's that?" he said, his voice bleary with sleep.

Suddenly Knuckles's voice rang out along the pipe on the wall.

"Paddington? Paddington!" Knuckles called urgently.

Paddington opened a vent so he could hear better. "What's up?" he asked.

"Ah, good. You're awake. Got a proposition for you, kid," said Knuckles. "Me and the boys have been talking. It seems to us that, if you're going to clear your name, you're going to need our help."

Phibs's voice joined in. "The Browns may mean well but—"

Spoon took up the thread. "It takes a thief to catch a thief."

Knuckles agreed. "If the three of us were to get out of here," he went on, "we could hit the streets together and we'd soon find him."

Paddington was horrified. "You're not talking about escape?"

"We certainly are," said Knuckles. "And we've got a plan, but it's a four-man job and we need your help. What do you say?"

Paddington felt sorely tempted. He had well and truly had enough of his cell. But escaping? He wasn't sure about that. When it came down to it, he just wasn't that kind of bear.

"It's very kind of you, Knuckles," he said, "but I don't think Aunt Lucy would like the idea of me breaking out of prison."

"But you're innocent," Knuckles reminded him.

"I know—but *you're* not!" said Paddington. "You robbed a bank."

"That's not fair!" said Knuckles, sounding hurt. "I did leave an IOU note."

"And I'm a locksmith by trade," said Spoon. "I just so happen to like practicing at night on jewelry shops."

"And I've always wanted to fly an airplane," said

Phibs. "Is that a crime?"

"It is if you steal it," said Paddington. "Look, I know you mean well, but the Browns will take me home in the end, you'll see," he said.

There was a pause and Paddington thought the others had gone.

Then Knuckles said quietly, "You may not want to hear this, kid, but sooner or later the Browns will give up on you."

Paddington felt his stomach churn as he listened to the other prisoners back Knuckles up.

"When they don't find that thief," said Phibs, "they'll start to question your story."

"They'll miss one visit, then two . . . ," said Spoon.

"And before you know it," finished Knuckles, "they'll have abandoned you altogether."

Paddington was affronted by this. "You're wrong," he said. "You're *all* wrong. The Browns aren't like that. They'll come tomorrow and they'll have good news, you'll see."

He closed the vent very firmly.

But, as he tried to get back to sleep, he couldn't get Knuckles's words out of his head.

Paddington needn't have worried. Ever since Mrs. Brown had come back from Phoenix's house, she and the children had been busy plotting with Mrs. Bird. They felt sure they had come up with a master plan that would catch the devious actor red-handed and allow Paddington to finally come home to his family.

The first part of the plan had Judy and Jonathan traveling across London to the office of Flick Fanshawe, Phoenix Buchanan's agent.

They rushed up to the door of Flick's office and pressed a buzzer next to her name.

Judy leaned in and spoke into the intercom. "Good morning," she said. "This is Judy Brown from the *Portobello Express*. I have an appointment."

The door clicked open and Judy and Jonathan climbed the stairs to Flick Fanshawe's office. They knocked on the door.

"Come in!" a voice called out.

Judy went in first. The office was a large room with theater posters and photographs of actors up on the walls. Flick herself sat behind an enormous desk. She stood up when the children came in and held out a well-manicured hand.

Flick flashed her white teeth in a dazzling smile. "What's this for, darlings? A school newspaper, you say?"

"That's right," said Judy.

Jonathan put a Dictaphone on the desk and pressed

"Record" while Judy explained.

"We're doing a career profile," Judy was saying. "We thought an interview with the agent of THE Phoenix Buchanan would be really interesting. Oh, and we brought these with us, by the way," she said, offering Flick a basket of Chelsea buns. "As a thank-you for seeing us at such short notice."

"Lovely!" said Flick. She took one. "I'm sure an interview with me would be just the thing for your little newspaper. Inspiring to the kiddies, no doubt! Right, I've only got two minutes, so we'd better make it snappy," she said, biting into the bun. "Hmm. Nice buns by the way."

Not wanting to waste a moment, Jonathan jumped in with a question. "When can we expect to see Mr. Buchanan back on stage?"

"Phoenix?" Flick said through a mouthful of crumbs. "I wouldn't hold your breath, darling. Don't get me wrong, he's a *fantastic* actor but he's got one teensy-weensy problem, which is that he won't work with other actors—thinks they 'dilute his talent'—" She broke off to check the time on her expensive watch. "Ooh, look! I must scoot," she cried. "We're having lunch with a big Broadway producer." She finished off the Chelsea bun and leaped from her chair.

"A Broadway producer? That sounds exciting," said Judy. She was desperate to try to delay the agent from leaving right away. "Where are you going?"

"Where do you think? Where do all the big meetings happen? The Ritz, darling!" said Flick, taking another bun. "Hmm," she said, munching away. "*Really* nice buns. Got to fly! Byeee!" she called out over her shoulder.

Judy and Jonathan exchanged a devious smile and Jonathan pressed "Stop" on the Dictaphone.

"Did you get everything we need?" Judy asked in a low voice.

"I think so," said Jonathan. "I hope Mum's managed to carry out her part of the plan."

Mrs. Brown was indeed doing her bit back in Windsor Gardens. She had Mrs. Bird to help her too.

To any passerby, it would seem that Mrs. Bird was having an innocent chat with the postman. In reality, however, she was causing a diversion so that Mrs. Brown could carry out her plan unnoticed.

"Good morning, Marlon!"

"Good morning, Mrs. B. How's Paddington doing?" the postman asked.

"Oh, he's a tough wee bear," said Mrs. Bird.

She kept the postman chatting while Mrs. Brown took

advantage of the diversion to sneak round the side of the van with a large hamper from Barkridges' department store. She quickly checked around her to make sure the coast was clear, then climbed inside the hamper. Just as the postman finished his chat with Mrs. Bird, Mrs. Brown pulled the lid down so that she was completely hidden.

"Better get on," said the postman, waving goodbye to Mrs. Bird.

He walked round to the side of his van and spotted the hamper.

"Who's this for, then?" he asked himself, reading the address label. "Mr. Buchanan? Okay. Off we go. Phew, it's heavy!" he muttered.

Heaving the hamper on to a trolley, the postman wheeled it round to Phoenix Buchanan's door and rang the bell.

Mrs. Bird was spying from a phone booth.

She waited as Phoenix opened the door, looked delightedly at the hamper, and took it safely inside his house. Then, quickly checking to make sure no one was watching her, Mrs. Bird picked up the receiver and dialed.

In a different phone booth, on the other side of town, Judy and Jonathan were waiting too—for Mrs. Bird to call them! As soon as the phone rang, Judy answered it. Jonathan squeezed in alongside his sister so that he could hear what Mrs. Bird had to say.

"The parcel has been delivered," said Mrs. Bird in a cryptic tone. "I repeat: the parcel has been delivered."

Judy said nothing in response. She simply replaced the receiver and then went to dial a new number . . .

Inside Phoenix's house, he was settling down to open the hamper.

"Oh, this is exciting," he said to himself. "I wonder if it's from a fan—" He was stopped from opening it up fully, however, by the phone ringing.

"Oh! A hamper *and* a phone call in one morning. Popular little me!" he trilled as he went to answer.

"Hello?" he said. "Phoenix Buchanan. Star of the stage and screen—"

"Phoenix!"

"Flick? Is that you?" Phoenix asked. "It's not every day I hear from my agent." He sounded grumpy. "I hope it's good news—"

The voice on the other end cut in. *"I've only got two minutes, so we'd better make it snappy."* It was Flick's voice—but it wasn't really her. It was the recording that Jonathan had made when he and Judy were in Flick's office earlier!

"Okay," said Phoenix, believing it to be the agent herself. "But it better *had* be good. You haven't got me any work apart from that dreadful dog-food commercial for years."

"*We're having lunch with a big Broadway producer,*" said his agent's voice.

Phoenix's mood changed dramatically. He gasped in delight. "That's wonderful! Where should I meet you?"

"*Where do all the big meetings happen? The Ritz, darling!*"

"I'm on my way!" Phoenix cried.

He was about to take the receiver away from his ear when he heard Flick's voice say, "*Nice buns by the way.*"

"I beg your pardon?" said Phoenix.

Back in the phone booth, Judy and Jonathan looked at each other aghast—had they given the game away?

"*Really nice buns!*" Flick's voice said.

"Well, thank you very much," said Phoenix, plainly flattered.

Judy and Jonathan let out the breath they had been holding and looked hugely relieved. "I think we got away with it!" Judy whispered as she replaced the receiver.

Phoenix put his phone down and checked out his rear view in a mirror. "Nice buns, eh? Well, I've certainly never had any complaints about Mr. and Mrs. Botty-Cheek," he said to his reflection.

Then, with a laugh, he ran to what he thought was a very important appointment at the Ritz.

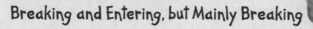

CHAPTER 17

Breaking and Entering, but Mainly Breaking

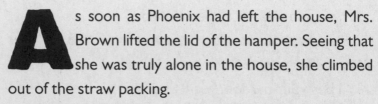

As soon as Phoenix had left the house, Mrs. Brown lifted the lid of the hamper. Seeing that she was truly alone in the house, she climbed out of the straw packing.

"Urgh. It was hot in there," she muttered. "And if anyone had said one more time how heavy I was . . ."

She went immediately to a pile of Phoenix's personal papers and began riffling through for anything that might provide a clue about the whereabouts of the pop-up book.

"What's this?" she said under her breath. She had unearthed a notebook. It was blank, but she could see some faint marks left by a pen. "Someone has written on the previous page and torn it out," she said to herself.

Thinking quickly, Mrs. Brown took a pencil from her hair and shaded over the invisible writing. The words emerged in the gray shading: *Saturday 06:35 Where All Your Dreams Come True.*

"What can that mean?" Mrs. Brown asked herself, chewing the end of the pencil. She was deep in thought when a sharp knock at the window startled her.

Mrs. Brown almost jumped out of her skin. Her hands flew to her throat and her heart clamored in her chest.

She looked up anxiously and then sighed irritably. It was her husband!

She opened the window. "Henry? What are you doing?" she said, looking out into the street to check that Phoenix had definitely gone.

"What are *you* doing, more like?" Mr. Brown asked. "Have you gone insane?"

It was then that Mrs. Brown saw what her husband was wearing.

"I could ask you the same question. Why are you wearing your pajamas?" she exclaimed.

Mr. Brown looked defensive. "I was having a lazy morning," he said. "More to the point, I looked out of the window and saw you in HERE. I rushed over straight-away to stop you from doing anything stupid. This is breaking and entering, you know," he added, climbing in through the open window.

Mrs. Brown turned away and resumed her hunt for clues. "We haven't broken anything," she said.

Mr. Brown immediately bumped into a large vase, knocked it over, and broke it. "Good grief!" he exclaimed, sweeping at the broken pieces. "Look at the mess you've got us into! I wish you hadn't started this wild-goose chase. Give me one reason why Phoenix Buchanan would steal a pop-up book? He's already a millionaire."

"*Was* a millionaire," Mrs. Brown corrected her husband, ignoring his panicky cries. "He owes money all over town—he hasn't got a penny to his name." She held up a handful of unpaid bills.

"So, he has a lot of red bills," said Mr. Brown impatiently. "Everyone does . . . Goodness me," he said, picking up an invoice from the pile. "The man spends a lot on face cream!"

"Come on," said Mrs. Brown urgently. "We need to find that book and get out of here before Phoenix comes back. We haven't much time."

"So where next?" asked Mr. Brown.

"Let's go upstairs . . . ," said Mrs. Brown, already running up the stairs.

"Look!" she said, pointing at two indentations in the carpet on the landing. "Marks where a ladder has been."

"You really have been reading too many detective novels, Mary," Mr. Brown muttered.

Mrs. Brown merely smiled as she pointed at a hatch door above their heads. "Give me a leg up!" she said.

Mr. Brown did as he was asked, with much muttering and complaining. In seconds his wife had swung open the hatch to reveal a folded-up stepladder. "Carefully does it," said Mr. Brown as his wife pulled the ladder down.

It landed neatly in the marks on the landing carpet.

"I knew he would have a secret room hidden away," Mrs. Brown breathed.

"It's not a secret room; it's an attic. Everyone in the street has one," said Mr. Brown, rolling his eyes. Nonetheless, he followed his wife up the ladder.

Mrs. Brown flicked a light switch and gasped at what she saw: the costumed mannequins leered at her in the gloom, lending the room a distinctly spooky air.

Mr. Brown took one look at them and shuddered. "Good grief. He's a weirdo," he said.

Mrs. Brown pointed at the costumes. "Look, Henry!" she said in a whisper. "The nun . . . the thief . . . the king . . ."

Mr. Brown's jaw dropped. "Phoenix *is* the thief. We were right!"

"WE?" Mrs. Brown exclaimed hotly.

"Well, I never said—" Mr. Brown began. But he stopped when he heard a noise. "Shh!" he said, tiptoeing toward the open hatch and listening intently. "I think I heard the front door open."

Mr. Brown had heard correctly. Phoenix Buchanan had forgotten his favorite cravat and come back to fetch it.

"I need to look even more gorgeous than usual for this important lunch," he said to himself as he came in through the front door.

"Quick!" Mrs. Brown whispered. "Let's get out of here."

They crept down the ladder from the attic and closed the hatch behind them. Mrs. Brown beckoned to her husband to come to the banister and together they peered over.

"He's gone into the kitchen," Mr. Brown whispered.

They stole down the stairs and along the hallway as quietly as they could. Just as they reached the front door they heard Phoenix come out of the kitchen. Quick as a flash Mrs. Brown darted into the living room, dragging her husband with her.

Phoenix was on his way back out and hadn't heard a thing, But then he happened to notice the living-room door was open.

"I'm sure I shut that behind me when I left," he said to himself. He peered into the room and spotted the broken vase. "Intruder!" he gasped, ducking back into the hall. He nipped over to a suit of armor stand-ing against the wall and took an ornamental sword from the gloved hand.

"Hello, who's there?" he called out, brandishing the sword.

There was no noise or movement from anywhere in the house.

Phoenix crept back into the living room.

At first glance everything seemed normal.

Then Phoenix saw Mr. Brown's legs disappearing behind the sofa.

"Henry?" said Phoenix, puzzled. "Is that you?" He let the arm holding the sword fall to his side.

Mr. Brown sheepishly got to his feet. "Ah, hello, Phoenix," he said. He glanced down, noticing the weapon in Phoenix's hand, and his legs began to shake.

"What on earth are you doing here?" Phoenix asked.

Mr. Brown pulled himself up to his full height and made an effort to take control of the situation. "I might ask you the same thing," he said.

"I live here!" Phoenix exclaimed.

"And I"—Mr. Brown hesitated, looking for the right words—"insure it," he said. Feeling emboldened by this excuse, he continued. "And for my company's Platinum Club members we perform a full home inspection to verify your security arrangements."

Phoenix eyed him doubtfully. "In your pajamas?"

"Hmm-mm," said Mr. Brown, not trusting himself to say more.

"With your wife?" Phoenix added, his voice heavy with skepticism. He pulled back the curtain to reveal Mrs. Brown, who was pretending to inspect the security of the windows by tapping the glass.

"Ah, good. Seems pretty safe," she said hastily. Then turning to face the others she feigned surprise. "Oh, hi, Phoenix! I didn't hear you come in."

"You see?" Mr. Brown said to Phoenix. "Mary helps me out from time to time."

Phoenix narrowed his eyes. "We-ell," he said slowly, "I must say that sounds . . . plausible."

"Does it?" said Mr. Brown brightly. "Great. Well, I'm delighted to say we can give you a clean bill of health. I'll get the chaps in the office to type up the paperwork ASAP."

"Wonderful," said Phoenix, smiling thinly.

"Good," said Mr. Brown. "Well, we'd better get cracking. Come on, Mary."

Phoenix saw them out to the door.

Mr. Brown turned on the doorstep and said, "Cheerio! Hope to see you soon, Phoenix."

"Maybe not in your—erm—pajamas next time?" the actor replied.

They all laughed and the Browns made a swift get-away.

Phoenix watched them very carefully as they went.

As soon as the Browns had left, Phoenix shot upstairs and scrambled up the ladder to his attic room. He frantically checked his belongings and was relieved to find that the pop-up book was still where he had left it.

"Thank goodness it's safe," said Phoenix. Opening the precious book, he stood dramatically, legs wide, as though onstage. Then, addressing one of his mannequins, he said, "Hold your nerve, Macbeth. Screw your courage to the sticking post. We are almost there. I have followed this little lady all the way across London and found every one of her clever little clues."

He smiled down at the picture of the tiny trapeze artist, then frowned, deep in thought. "But what on earth do they mean?" he muttered. "It's just a jumble of letters. If only Grandfather were here now to tell me himself."

He glanced across at another mannequin. "What would you say, Monsieur Poirot?" he asked, as though the famous detective were really standing before him. "Letters . . . what can letters mean? A code? A key . . . ? A key! That's it! They are not letters at all—they are musical notes!"

Phoenix's eyes shone in the gloom as he realized what he had just discovered. "If they *are* musical notes, there is only one place they will be of any use," he said. "And I am the only one who knows the truth! Without this book, the Browns have no proof. And by the time they get back, Phoenix Buchanan will have disappeared! Now be quiet, all of you," he said to the mannequins sternly. "I must prepare . . ."

And with that he sat down at his mirror and began applying makeup.

130

CHAPTER 18

Paddington and the Great Escape

Later that day, the Browns and Mrs. Bird went to the police station with the evidence Mrs. Brown had gathered. They told the officer on duty all about Phoenix and the costumes in his attic and explained that they believed him to be the true thief of the pop-up book.

The officer took notes, while looking extremely skeptical.

"I know what you are thinking, Officer," said Mr. Brown. "My wife is insane."

"Thank you, darling," said Mrs. Brown with a thin smile.

"But she was right all along," Mr. Brown persisted.

Jonathan chipped in. "Judy's the only person who's been printing the truth," he said, holding up one of his sister's newspapers.

Judy blushed. "Jonathan helped me," she said.

"But don't tell anyone," Jonathan pleaded. "Not cool."

"All right, that is an amazing story," said the police-woman, holding up a hand to stop them. "But all you've proved is that Phoenix Buchanan keeps his old costumes in an attic room. I need solid proof that he is the thief. Bring me the pop-up book with Phoenix's fingerprints on it, and then we can talk."

"But—" said Jonathan.

"Until then there's nothing I can do," said the police-woman firmly. "I am sorry," she said, walking away from the Browns.

Mrs. Brown looked horrified. "Where's she going?" she said.

"What are we going to do now?" Jonathan asked.

"I don't know," said Mrs. Brown sadly.

Mrs. Bird tried to cheer everyone up. "At least we can tell Paddington we know who did it now," she said. "That should give him hope."

As she said this, the clock struck three.

"Oh NO!" they cried, looking at each other in horror. "We've missed visiting hour!"

While the Browns had been trying to clear Paddington's name, Paddington had been waiting anxiously for his visitors, Knuckles's words still ringing in his ears.

Before you know it, they'll have abandoned you alto-gether . . .

"The Browns won't forget me," Paddington told himself. He repeated it over and over, but as he sat and waited and watched the other prisoners' visitors come and go, he realized that Knuckles may well have been right.

At three o'clock the klaxon sounded to signal the end of visiting time. Poor Paddington gave a soft growl of despair. He left the room as all the lights in the visitors' booths went out.

He went back to his cell and lay on his bed, looking at the photo of himself with the Browns and Mrs. Bird. He tried to imagine the photo with him no longer in it. . . . As he did so, he shed a single tear, which fell to the floor of Paddington's cell and soaked into the floorboards.

Paddington sat, staring at the patch where the tear had fallen. It made him think of the first raindrops in the forest back in Darkest Peru during the tropical storms. He stared at the watermark and imagined the teardrop producing a single green shoot that grew up and up. Soon, in his mind's eye, his cell had disappeared and he was looking at the Peruvian rain forest that had once been his home. And there was his dear Aunt Lucy calling his name. If ever he needed her guidance, now was the time . . .

"Aunt Lucy! Aunt Lucy!" It was really her!

"Paddington!" She drew her nephew toward her in a warm embrace. "What are you doing here?" she asked. "I thought you'd be at home."

Paddington pulled away from her and looked into her eyes. "I'm afraid I don't have a home anymore," he said miserably. "You see, I'm in prison and even the Browns have forgotten me."

Aunt Lucy said nothing. In fact, as Paddington looked at her, she faded from view and the jungle around her disappeared.

There was a knocking sound and Paddington realized another voice was calling him now—a voice that was not his aunt's. It brought him back to the stark reality of his cell.

"Paddington!" It was Knuckles calling down the pipes again. "Tonight's the night. If you want to clear your name, it's now or never. You in?"

Paddington leaned against the pipes. He tried to swallow the lump that had formed in this throat.

"Yes," he said reluctantly. "I'm in."

Later that evening, after the warden called for "lights-out," Phibs, Spoon, Knuckles, and Paddington each lifted the floorboards of their cells and dropped down to an

134

underfloor passage. They met up and crawled in a line to the end of the prison building.

"Down the laundry chute, boys," said Knuckles, taking the lead.

The prisoners followed him one by one, whizzing down the chute like a giant slide and landing on a pile of dirty clothes at the bottom.

"To the pigeonholes!" said Knuckles. "You know what to do."

Paddington and the men went to find their own clothes and possessions. Then Paddington, as he was the smallest, was chosen to climb up inside the clock tower so that he could sneak into the warden's office and take the key to the canteen, from where they could make their escape. Luckily he had always been good at climbing, thanks to spending his cubhood in the treetops of Darkest Peru. He clambered up through the clockwork and managed to tiptoe to the rack where the warden kept his keys. Then he scurried back to meet the others.

Paddington and his friends made a beeline for the canteen, where they took a huge bundle of tablecloths that had been stitched together to form one enormous sheet of fabric.

Knuckles shimmied out of a skylight above the kitchen, while the other prisoners passed him the tablecloth, a laundry basket, and some canisters of propane gas. Then they all climbed out after Knuckles.

A searchlight swept across the roof. The prisoners waited for it to pass them by, then ran over the roof to the shadows at the base of the prison watchtower.

"Open the laundry basket," said Knuckles. They opened out the huge tablecloth and fixed it by its edges to the sides of the basket.

"Light the propane!" Knuckles commanded.

Phibs put the canister into the middle of the basket and then opened the gas valve while Spoon lit it. A tall orange flame shot up and the tablecloth began to rise.

"Hop in!" shouted Knuckles.

Paddington, Spoon, and Phibs followed Knuckles's lead and leaped into the basket, just as the tablecloth inflated fully.

Inside the prison, T-Bone was gazing out of his tiny cell window. He almost fell over in shock at what he saw.

"A hot-air balloon?" he said, shaking his head as though to get rid of a dream. But he wasn't imagining things. There really was a hot-air balloon rising from the prison watchtower! A hot-air balloon made from some tablecloths and a laundry basket. And carrying three men and a bear.

"Well, blow me down," T-Bone said to himself as he

watched the prisoners rise up into the sky. "Good luck, young bear," he whispered.

All three men threw their prison caps into the air and whooped with delight as the balloon rose higher and higher. Paddington was quiet, however. He looked out over the city he loved, and worried about the choice he had made.

What would Aunt Lucy have to say about me being a fugitive? he thought anxiously.

The balloon floated out over the Docklands. By now the prisoners had changed into their own clothing and ditched their prison uniforms. Paddington tried to console himself that at least he felt more comfortable in his old hat and duffle coat. And it was a relief to be reunited with his trusty suitcase.

The balloon traveled fast. Soon Knuckles was asking Spoon to take them down.

"We're there, boys!" he said, looking over the edge.

Spoon cut the flame and the balloon began to drift to the ground. It came to rest by a derelict factory in the East End of London. As the giant tablecloth deflated, the prisoners climbed out of the basket and ran to a nearby wharf. Using the wall of a warehouse as cover, they crept along until they reached a gate.

Knuckles said, "Stop! There she is . . ." He pointed through the gate. "Our ticket out of here."

Paddington followed the prisoners' gaze. His eyes settled on a seaplane. "What's this?" he asked, startled. "Aren't you taking me back to the Browns' house? Where are you going?"

The prisoners looked at one another guiltily.

"Aren't we going to clear my name?" Paddington persisted. "I thought that was the plan."

Knuckles looked sheepish. "Sorry, kid," he said, "but the plan has changed."

"We're leaving the country," said Spoon. "We thought you'd like to come with us."

"But you said . . . You lied to me!" Paddington exclaimed. He couldn't believe what he was hearing.

Knuckles looked very ashamed. "It's not like that," he protested weakly. "We've done you a favor really. If we'd told you the truth, you'd never have come along. It's better this way," he said.

Paddington frowned. "I thought you were my friends," he said quietly.

"We are," said Phibs, looking upset.

"We'll find someplace nobody knows us and start again," Knuckles assured him. "And we'll make marmalade together." He rubbed his hands. "We'll make a fortune."

Paddington shook his head. "But I don't want to leave the country, Knuckles. I want to go and clear my name and go back to live with the Browns. You said you'd help me."

"I'm sorry, kid," said Knuckles, spreading his huge hands. "I also said I don't do nuthin' for no one for nuthin'."

Paddington dropped his head. Then, taking one last look at the prisoners, he turned and ran.

"Where are you going?" Phibs called after him.

"Paddington!" Spoon shouted.

But Paddington had already disappeared from sight.

CHAPTER 19

Paddington on the Run

Paddington ran until he could run no longer. He found himself on a busy main road and stopped to catch his breath just as a police car sped by. The sound of the siren made him jump—what if the police had discovered he was a fugitive and were after him already?

Paddington ducked out of sight down an alley, desperately looking for somewhere to hide. Then he spotted a phone booth and had an idea.

I wonder . . . he thought, putting his hand in his duffle-coat pocket. "There!" he said, bringing out the coin that Mrs. Bird had pulled from his ear all those months ago.

He dialed the Browns' number, praying that they would be at home—and that they would want to speak to him.

The pips went and Paddington put his coin in the slot.

"Hello!" Jonathan's voice rang out loud and clear.

Paddington was so excited that he started to speak right away. "Hello, Jonathan! It's Padd—"

But Jonathan's voice cut him off. "You've reached the Brown residence!"

Then Judy's voice said, "We're not in, but please leave a message . . ."

Then the answer phone beeped. Paddington slumped against the phone. He hadn't got through to the Browns after all—it was merely their answering machine.

"Hello," he said wearily. "It's me, Paddington. I hope you don't mind my calling." He imagined his voice echoing out down the empty hallway of 32 Windsor Gardens— his old home. "I just wanted to let you know that I've broken out of prison and, well, I suppose I'm on the run. I didn't really mean to, but Knuckles said that if we broke out he would help me clear my name and then I could come home. But he's gone now, and I'm on my own. I don't really know why I'm calling, but I suppose I just wanted to say . . . goodbye."

If only he'd known that the Browns has been out all night, putting up yet more posters in an attempt to bring him home. But Paddington had no idea that the Browns still cared about him, and so he put the receiver down. He slowly turned and opened the door of the phone booth. He stared at the ground, his shoulders drooping. The wind was getting up, and it was cold and dreary. Where was he going to go now? Would he ever find another family like the Browns? He began to trudge down the road, his paws sunk deep into his duffle-coat pockets. He could not remember ever feeling this miserable.

Just as he had given up all hope, he heard the sound of a phone ringing. He looked up. It was coming from the telephone booth where he had made his call to the Browns! Without stopping to think, Paddington raced back to answer it.

"Paddington?" said an anxious, familiar voice.

"Mrs. Brown!" cried Paddington. "YES! YES, IT'S PADDINGTON!" He could hear the other members of the family rushing to the phone, all talking at once. "I'm so sorry I escaped, Mrs. Brown," he continued. "I thought you'd given up on me."

"We'd never give up on you, Paddington," said Mrs. Brown with feeling, "you must know that."

"Paddington," said Mr. Brown, speaking down the phone over his wife's shoulder. "It's so good to hear your voice."

Mrs. Bird joined in. "You're family!" she said. "Of course we haven't forgotten you."

"And we know who the thief was," Paddington heard Judy say.

"It was Phoenix Buchanan," Jonathan added excitedly.

Paddington was puzzled. *"Mr. Buchanan?"* he repeated.

"That's right, dearie," said Mrs. Bird. "But he's disappeared into thin air."

Mrs. Brown took the phone back from the others. "We've been looking for him at every landmark in that book—every last page," she said with a sigh.

"Where all your dreams come true," said Paddington dreamily.

"Why do you say that?" asked Mrs. Brown.

"It was written on the back of the pop-up book," said Paddington. "That's why I thought it would be the perfect present for Aunt Lucy."

"I've seen those words before," said Judy.

"Where?" asked Jonathan.

"At the fair!" said Judy, sounding suddenly excited. "It was behind you, Paddington, when you helped Phoenix Buchanan open the fair. The fairground organ was behind you, and the words on the organ said 'Where All Your Dreams Come True.'"

"The organ . . ." said Jonathan, "that must be where Madame Kozlova hid her fortune."

"In that case, let's stop wasting time and get to the fair," said Mr. Brown in a businesslike manner.

"It's too late," said Mrs. Bird. "I read in the newspaper that they're leaving first thing in the morning."

"On their steam train?" asked Jonathan.

"Yes!" said Mrs. Brown. "The note! That must be where Phoenix is going at 06:35!"

Mr. Brown had clearly decided he needed to take control. "Paddington?" he said.

"Yes, Mr. Brown?" Paddington said eagerly.

"Get to the station right away. If we can find Phoenix and that book, we can prove everything. We'll meet you there!"

Paddington put down the receiver and rushed out of the phone booth. This time he was beaming from ear to ear. "The Browns didn't forget me," he said to himself. "And they are going to help me clear my name! I need to get to the railway station as fast as I can."

He stuck out a paw, trying to hitch a ride from passersby, but no one would stop for him. He tried again and again with no luck.

Just as he was about to give up hope, Fred Barnes the garbage collector came past.

"Mr. Barnes!" shouted Paddington. "You couldn't give me a lift, could you?"

"Paddington! Good to see you! 'Course I'll give you a lift," said Fred. "It's thanks to you I passed my exams. This is my last day on the bins—it's a cabbie's life for me. So, tell me, sir, where d'you want to go?" he asked with a grin.

"To the station!" cried Paddington. "As fast as you can!"

CHAPTER 20

Paddington Is on the Right Track

The Browns were in just as much of a hurry. They rushed out of 32 Windsor Gardens toward their car but Mr. Curry was blocking it. He was in his dressing gown and was holding a piece of cardboard that read "Neighborhood Watch Panic Levels." An arrow was pointing to the highest level of panic on the board and Mr. Curry was emphasizing this state of emergency by shouting at his neighbors through a bullhorn.

"Fellow citizens," he was saying, "this is your Community Defense Force commander."

All the neighbors were now coming to their windows to see what the noise was about.

"I have just received intelligence that the bear has escaped from prison," Mr. Curry went on importantly. "He may be heading this way. I am therefore raising the panic level to 'wild hysteria.'" He held the board up so that everyone could see.

"Please be quiet, Mr. Curry," said Mrs. Brown irritably.

"Paddington is not heading this way," said Judy, standing up to Mr. Curry with her mother.

"That's right," said Jonathan. "He's going to clear his name."

"And we're going to bring him home," said Mrs. Bird. She glared at Mr. Curry.

"Well, we don't want him here!" The indignant neighbor looked disgusted at the idea.

Mr. Brown went right up to Mr. Curry and looked him squarely in the eye. "Of course you don't. You never have. You took one look at that bear and you made up your mind. Well, Paddington's not like that. He looks for the good in all of us and somehow finds it. He wouldn't hesitate if any of *us* needed help. So stand aside, Mr. Curry. Because we're coming through."

Mr. Brown jumped into the car, his family just behind him. He put his key in the ignition and turned it to start the engine, but nothing happened.

"Come on, come on!" Mr. Brown urged the car. He was about to give up when suddenly it started to move.

The children and Mrs. Brown looked around to see that the neighbors were out in force and were pushing the car forward.

"Get back into your homes!" exclaimed Mr. Curry. "I am *ordering* you to get back to your homes."

Everyone ignored Mr. Curry.

"Go and bring Paddington back safely," cried Dr. Jafri, waving the Browns off.

The car roared to life and zoomed toward the kiosk. Mr. Curry jumped out of the way. His panic board was knocked flying as the Browns and Mrs. Bird rushed out of the street on their way to the station.

Paddington was having the ride of his life in the garbage truck. Fred sped along the streets and through the underpass where the walls of the tunnel were lined with posters saying "Free Paddington!" As Paddington watched them fly past, his heart was filled with joy.

The truck reached the rail station at last and Paddington hopped down.

"Here, put this on," said Fred. He pulled the black cover off a station trash can and popped it over Paddington as a disguise. It was just the right size for a small bear. "Off you go," said Fred. "Just remember— you're a bin! And watch out for coppers. Good luck!"

Paddington thanked his friend and began a funny hopping journey toward the station.

"You're a bin, you're a bin. Just an ordinary bin going for a walk," he muttered as he went.

He froze when he spotted a policeman at a cake stall just outside the doors. The man didn't notice him, though. He was too busy eating a doughnut. As he passed Paddington, the policeman dropped the remains of his snack into Paddington's trash can!

"Thank you!" called Paddington politely.

"You're welcome," said the policeman, not seeming to notice anything odd about a talking trash can.

Paddington breathed again and waited until the coast was clear before scuttling into the station. He hopped to the fairground steam train, which was already waiting to leave. Then he stopped and watched as a train porter approached the train.

Paddington gasped as he saw that this porter was, in fact, none other than Phoenix Buchanan in disguise! Phoenix made a convincing porter as he strutted along the platform. He clearly thought he looked very fine in the uniform too. He strode forth toward the steam train, then with a glance over his shoulder hopped into a carriage in the middle of the train.

Paddington was also checking that the coast was clear. Once he was sure it was safe to do so, he cast off his disguise and jumped onto the rear of the steam train. He was just in time—the minute he did this the guard blew a whistle and the train began to pull out of the station.

The Browns arrived on the platform just as Paddington's train was leaving.

"We're too late!" cried Mrs. Brown. "Look!"

"Never say never," said Mr. Brown. He looked very determined. "Come on. We can make it if we run."

Mrs. Brown and the others ran after him.

"We're right behind you, Mary," said Mrs. Bird, doing her best to keep up.

The train began to pick up speed as the Browns and Mrs. Bird raced along the platform. They ran faster and faster. Mr. Brown reached out his hand and almost touched the last carriage . . . But the train put on a burst of speed and chugged away.

"No!" cried Judy and Jonathan.

"We've *got* to catch up with that train," said Mrs. Brown.

"How are we going to do that?" asked Mr. Brown.

As if in answer, there was a whistle from a different train on the platform behind.

"Wow," said Jonathan, turning to see. "It's the Belmond British Pullman. Cool!"

Judy gave him a funny look, but she followed his gaze

to a magnificent old steam train on the next platform.

"That gives me an idea," said Jonathan. "Follow me!" He sneaked on board the train and beckoned to his family to do the same. The others didn't stop to ask why—they didn't have time if they were going to save Paddington.

Meanwhile Knuckles and his fellow prisoners were flying the seaplane high over the countryside. Knuckles tuned a portable radio to get the news.

"Four convicts made a daring escape from Portobello Prison last night," said the newsreader. *"So far the police have no clue as to the whereabouts of any of the prisoners . . ."*

Knuckles, Spoon, and Phibs cheered!

". . . except Paddington Brown," said the newsreader, *"who was last seen boarding a train bound for Bristol. The police are closing in."*

Their faces fell.

"Poor little guy," said Phibs glumly. "He must be somewhere down there now. Probably scared half to death."

Spoon caught Knuckles's eye. "Shouldn't we help him, Knuckles?"

"If we go down there now, they won't just lock us up; they'll throw away the key!"

"I know," said Spoon, "but he's our friend."

"We stick to the plan," Knuckles said fiercely. "I don't do nuthin' for no one for nuthin'." But the tough man had to turn away as he said this, so that his friends wouldn't see his eyes fill with tears.

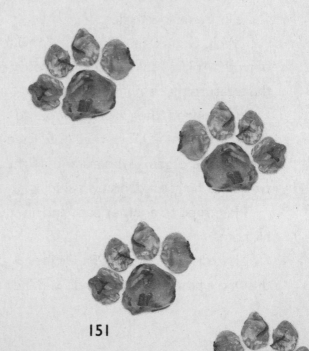

CHAPTER 21

A Sinking Feeling

Somewhere far below the seaplane the fairground train was rushing through the countryside. Phoenix Buchanan was taking off his porter's wig as he made his way to the carriage with the organ, clutching the pop-up book close to his chest. The organ was covered with tarpaulin. Phoenix pulled it off and gazed at the instrument with glee.

"Well, Grandfather," he said, "now for the moment of truth. At last I shall finish what you started and claim the treasure that is rightfully mine."

He opened the pop-up book to the first page. "'Tower Bridge—D,'" he read out. Then he pressed the note on the organ keyboard and a light appeared. "It's working!" he gasped, his eyes shining.

He turned to another page and another, keying in all his notes.

Little did he know that Paddington was watching him the whole time through a window in the carriage behind.

Paddington thought of Mr. Brown's words: *If we can find Phoenix and that book, we can prove everything.*

"But how am I going to do it?" Paddington asked himself. He looked around for inspiration and spotted a barrel of toffee apples. "Aha!" he said. "Something sticky—just what I need."

Taking one in each paw, he climbed up a ladder at the end of the carriage and clambered onto the windy roof. He needed to reach the skylight above Phoenix's head. Paddington breathed in sharply as he saw the train was about to go through a tunnel. He ducked down just in time and held on for dear life as the train went rocketing through it and out the other side.

Thinking on his paws, Paddington stuck the toffee apples to his feet, then using them as suckers so that he wasn't blown clean away he made his way across the roof.

Phoenix was pressing the last two notes in the code. "F . . ." he said, "and E . . ."

Suddenly the whole instrument lit up. Phoenix gazed at the organ, transfixed, while behind him Paddington swung through the skylight, using the toffee apples to hang from the ceiling above.

There was a whirring noise as all the cogs in the organ began to turn. The front of the instrument itself then began to open slowly, exposing a complex clockwork mechanism in the heart of the organ.

Phoenix's eyes grew wide with greed. "Soon the treasure will be mine!" he said.

Paddington was watching the whole thing. He chose his moment with care, waiting until Phoenix was distracted by the whirring cogs. Then he stretched down to grab the pop-up book from the actor's hands. He was almost there—but just not close enough to touch it! He inched forward on his sticky paws, stretching toward the book . . .

Phoenix was still entranced; the organ was completely open now. He gazed on the clockwork mechanism as, with more clicking and whirring, a gorgeous, intricately decorated treasure box rose up from somewhere deep inside the instrument.

Phoenix reached out his hands toward the object for which he had been hunting for so long. "Hello, my beauty!" he cried.

Paddington was near enough now to reach the pop-up book. He stretched as far as he could and succeeded at last in grabbing the book. Then he turned and began making his way slowly and stickily back to the skylight.

Just then, the box opened, revealing its treasure.

"Aren't you pretty?" said Phoenix as he gazed into its mirrored interior. But something caught his eye in the reflection. Phoenix turned away from the box to see Paddington hanging from the roof above him.

"YOU!" he shouted. He leaped up to grab the pop-up book from Paddington's paws; however, instead he succeeded in pulling Paddington back into the carriage with him.

The two of them collapsed in a heap, knocking against the keyboard of the organ.

The bump caused the pipes to descend and the treasure box began folding back into the instrument.

"NO!" groaned Phoenix, lunging for the treasure.

But it was too late. It had disappeared back inside the mechanism.

Paddington took advantage of the distraction to grab the pop-up book again. He turned and ran out of the carriage and through the train, leaving Phoenix to try to key in the code again from memory.

"D . . . G . . . ? No! E . . . G . . . ? NO! I'm never going to get it right without that book!"

With a howl of frustration the actor ran after Paddington. "Give me that book!" he yelled. "GIVE ME THAT BOOK!"

The Browns were catching up in their steam train with Jonathan at the helm. They were getting closer and closer to Paddington's train—but not close enough.

"Can this thing go any faster?" Mr. Brown asked Jonathan in despair.

"I can try to reroute the steam brake, but that'll take a couple of minutes," Jonathan shouted. "And we need more coal!"

"I'm on it!" said Mrs. Brown.

"Try to pull alongside," Mr. Brown said to Jonathan. "If you can line the front of our train up with the back of theirs, I'll be able to get across."

"I'll come with you, Dad," said Judy.

"Me too," said Mrs. Bird. "Just you try and stop us!" she added as Mr. Brown began to protest.

"Come on, then!" said Mr. Brown. And he swung out of the cab with the others close behind.

They made their way down to the front of their train while, inside, Mrs. Brown was furiously shoveling coal into the furnace to keep the train going and Jonathan was doing everything he could to get the steam train to move faster.

Judy, Mr. Brown, and Mrs. Bird had scrambled out onto the front of the engine by now. They were close enough to be able to climb across to the back of the fairground train. Mr. Brown helped Mrs. Bird and Judy across. He had one foot on each train and was about to clamber aboard and join the others when suddenly the tracks parted.

The two trains diverged and Mr. Brown found himself sliding as his legs moved farther and farther apart . . .

He closed his eyes and, remembering what his Chakrabatics instructor had taught him, he intoned, "Open your mind and your legs will follow."

His face took on a picture of pure peace as he meditated on this phrase. Then, as the trains moved even farther apart, Mr. Brown went into a split!

He opened his eyes, smiling with delight. "I've done it— Oh no!" he cried as he saw a bollard in the middle of the tracks, getting closer and closer toward him.

"Don't worry, dearie. I've got you!" shouted Mrs. Bird, leaning across and pulling him to safety on to the fairground train.

"Thank heaven for Chakrabatics!" Mr. Brown murmured, mopping his brow.

Paddington meanwhile was running down the fairground train looking for an escape. He scrambled out through a window and up on to the roof.

"I'm coming to get you!" Phoenix cried.

He climbed out of the carriage and chased Paddington across the roof.

"Where do you think you're going, Bear?" he shouted. "It's a train! It comes to an end—like all of us, alas," he added.

Paddington turned to see Phoenix gaining on him. He ran faster and faster until he realized Phoenix was right—he was nearly at the other end of the train! He skidded to a halt just as he reached the edge and wheeled back on his paws to prevent himself from falling.

"Whoops!" said Phoenix, striding toward Paddington.

Paddington's eyes grew wide in horror as Phoenix came closer and closer.

"Exit bear, pursued by an actor," said Phoenix, laughing. Then, "Whoops!" he cried again, as a skylight opened beneath him and he went tumbling into the carriage beneath.

He landed with a bump in front of Mrs. Bird, Judy, and Mr. Brown.

"Mrs. Bird?" said Phoenix, blinking up at her.

"Oh, you remember me now!" she scoffed.

Phoenix looked from Mrs. Bird to Judy and Mr. Brown. "The cavalry! An old crone, a little girl, and an insurance man. What are you going to do to me, Henry?" he teased.

Mr. Brown put up his fists and glowered at Phoenix.

"I'm going to bloomin' well biff you on the nose," he declared.

Phoenix raised an eyebrow and coolly grabbed a sword swallower's sword from the wall. He brandished it professionally at Henry. "Not a very good idea. I've got Stage Combat Level Four, you know."

Mr. Brown gulped and put his fists down.

Mrs. Bird had been looking around for a suitable weapon. She spotted a gun on a rack at her end of the carriage. "Where I come from, laddie," she said, grabbing the gun and pointing it at Phoenix, "they teach you not to bring a knife to a gunfight!" Judy and Mr. Brown gasped as Mrs. Bird took aim at Phoenix.

Phoenix smiled calmly. "I think you'll find that gun shoots only plastic darts."

Mrs. Bird pulled the trigger. Sure enough, a plastic dart hit Phoenix smack on the forehead.

He pulled it off with a pop, still smiling.

"So it does," said Mrs. Bird.

"Whereas this sword is razor sharp," said Phoenix. "Now, back you go," he added, waving the sword at them and grabbing some handcuffs from beside him.

By now, the two train lines were coming together again. Paddington glanced out between the two carriages to see the Pullman steam train pulling up alongside once more.

"Mrs. Brown!" he shouted.

Hearing his cry, Mrs. Brown stuck her head out of the driver's cab. "Paddington! Thank goodness. She turned back into the cab. "Jonathan, slow down."

"Okay, Mum!" he replied, putting on the brakes.

The trains were still at least ten yards apart, with no obvious way for Paddington to get across to Mrs. Brown and Jonathan.

"How am I going to do this?" Paddington asked himself. He looked around for something—anything—that he could use to bridge the gap between the two trains. His gaze fell on his trusty leather suitcase. And an idea began to form.

Paddington was not the only one struggling to escape. Phoenix had handcuffed Mr. Brown, Mrs. Bird, and Judy to some poles.

"Set us free!" Mr. Brown growled, wriggling.

Phoenix laughed. "I'll deal with you later. But first I'm going to sort out your furry friend . . ."

Paddington jammed the door of the adjoining carriage shut before opening his suitcase and pulling out his telescopic window-cleaning ladder. He began to unwind it so it extended toward the Pullman train.

He was just beginning to feel hopeful that his plan would work when Phoenix arrived outside the door and began kicking at it, trying to break it down.

Paddington jumped on to the front end of the ladder so that it took him with it as it stretched farther and farther across the gap between the trains. Paddington wound the handle faster still. He was almost across when Phoenix gave the door one last kick and the wood splintered . . .

Further back down inside the fairground train, Judy was panicking. "What are we going to do?" she cried, struggling to pull herself free from the handcuffs.

"Don't you worry, dearie," said Mrs. Bird. "I learned a trick or two from Harry Houdini, the famous escapologist . . ."

Phoenix was standing between his carriage and Paddington's. He had caught sight of the bear, who was still trying to make his way across the tracks on his telescopic ladder.

"Hello there," the actor called out. He smiled nastily. "What a clever little bear!" he said, realizing what

Paddington was trying to do.

Paddington didn't stop to respond to Phoenix, but kept inching nearer and nearer to Jonathan and Mrs. Brown.

Phoenix gave a wicked laugh, then leaned forward and pressed the "Retract" button on the ladder.

Paddington was immediately pinged back across the tracks.

"Whoooaah!" he shouted as he felt himself fly back into the arms of the evil actor.

"Thank you," said Phoenix, whipping the pop-up book out of Paddington's paws. Then he shoved the little bear into the final carriage of the train and slammed the door, throwing the bolts across for good measure.

"Let's see you get out of that!" he cried, pulling out the pin that joined Paddington's carriage to his own.

He leaned out of his carriage and used the pin to knock a trackside lever.

The points shifted and Paddington's carriage was disconnected and sent hurtling on to a different track.

"Bye-bye, Bear!" said Phoenix.

He turned back triumphant, but stopped dead when he saw he was surrounded by coconuts on stands. Facing him was Judy, her camera clicking away.

"Honestly, now's not the time for the paparazzi!"

said Phoenix, flashing her his best movie-star grin.

"On the contrary, it's perfect timing," said Mr. Brown. And he lifted his arm and hurled a ball straight at Phoenix's head.

Phoenix opened his mouth to cry out. But it was too late. Mr. Brown had knocked him out cold.

"Mr. Brown!" Paddington's desperate cries came floating through the window. "Help!"

Mr. Brown ran to the window, but all he could do was watch, helpless, as the runaway carriage crashed through the buffers at the end of the siding.

"NO!" yelled Henry.

Paddington's carriage went hurtling down a slope and into the murky waters of the river below.

Mrs. Brown was watching the whole disastrous scene from the Pullman train. "Stop the train, Jonathan!" she ordered.

Jonathan pulled hard on the brake lever.

The train shrieked to a halt while the fairground train hurtled off into the distance with Mr. Brown still on board.

Mrs. Brown jumped off and shouted to Jonathan to go and get help. She ran to the side of the bridge as Paddington's carriage began sinking into the river.

"I didn't do all that training in the Serpentine for

nothing," said Mrs. Brown defiantly. She pulled off her coat and dived into the water.

Inside the carriage, Paddington was pushing and pushing at the side door, but it wouldn't budge. Memories of being caught as a baby bear in the fast-flowing Amazon river came rushing back to him.

"I survived that," he told himself, trying to stay calm. "Aunt Lucy saved me." He shoved the door but still it wouldn't open. "But Aunt Lucy isn't here now."

It was no good. Paddington was starting to panic. He was struggling to breathe now in the few inches of air that had been trapped toward the top of the carriage. He had given up all hope and was sinking under the water.

This is it, he thought. *I'm sorry, Aunt Lucy. I'll never get you your perfect birthday present now . . .*

He turned for one final look through the window at the world above him, which was disappearing fast.

And then, suddenly, Mrs. Brown appeared, swimming toward the door! She was there to save him!

Paddington struggled to stay still so that he wouldn't use up the remaining air in the carriage. Meanwhile Mrs. Brown heaved the door open bit by bit. Paddington could see her face through a crack in the door, but it wouldn't open any further than that.

Mrs. Brown looked around frantically to see why the door wouldn't budge. Then she saw—it had been chained shut.

Paddington pushed at the door on his side while Mrs. Brown tugged on hers. They worked together with all their might but it was no good—the chain was just too strong.

Mrs. Brown reached her arm through the gap and took hold of Paddington's paw. They gazed at each other, knowing the end was near.

Then Mrs. Brown felt a huge meaty hand on her shoulder.

She looked round and saw to her delight that Knuckles, Phibs, and Spoon were there, right behind her.

Above them on the surface of the water was the silhouette of the seaplane. They had tracked Paddington down and followed him all the way. Together, the three men and Mary pulled at the door until the chain broke. Mrs. Brown reached in and pulled Paddington out.

They swam up, breaking through the surface of the water and gasping for breath.

"Thank goodness!" Mrs. Brown spluttered as they reached the bank. She helped Paddington out. "You all right there, Paddington?" she asked.

"I think so, Mrs. Brown," said Paddington shakily.

Knuckles, Phibs, and Spoon hauled themselves out of the water.

"Thank you for coming back, Knuckles," Paddington said to his friend. "But what made you change your mind?"

Knuckles smiled ruefully. "Can't make marmalade on my own now, can I?" he said.

Paddington gave a tired smile and immediately fainted.

Mrs. Brown gasped. She felt his forehead. "He's burning up," she said, looking at Knuckles in alarm.

"Best get the little fella to bed," said Knuckles tenderly.

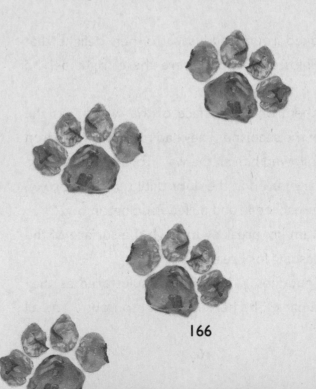

CHAPTER 22

Paddington and the Big Surprise

I t was three days before Paddington finally woke up. He blinked blearily. Everything was out of focus.

"Where am I?" he asked sleepily.

"Don't you exert yourself now," said Mrs. Bird, stroking his forehead.

Paddington opened his eyes properly. His face shone as he realized he was back in his own attic room. He looked around and saw that the whole family was there, waiting patiently for him to wake up.

"Paddington!" Judy exclaimed with joy.

"Take it easy now," said Mrs. Brown, laying a hand on his paw.

"You gave us a wee scare, but you're home now," said Mrs. Bird kindly.

"Home?" said Paddington. He tried to sit up.

"That's right," said Mrs. Brown.

Judy handed him a copy of her newspaper.

The headline read: "EXCLUSIVE! PADDINGTON FREED! ACTOR ARRESTED!"

"The police realized they'd made a terrible mistake," said Jonathan.

"Phoenix Buchanan has been sent to prison," Mr. Brown explained. "And, I might add, he's been thrown out of my company's Platinum Club."

"You're a free bear, Paddington," said Mrs. Bird.

Paddington smiled. "How long have I been asleep?" he asked.

"Three days!" Jonathan declared.

"Three *days*?" Paddington repeated. "But that means..."

"It's Aunt Lucy's birthday," said Judy, nodding.

The spark went out of Paddington's eyes. "Oh. And I never sent her anything," he said.

"It's all right, Paddington," said Mrs. Brown.

Paddington struggled to sit up again. "No, but you don't understand!" he protested. "Aunt Lucy gave up her dream of coming to London to look after me. I wanted to give her the pop-up book as a small way of making her dream come true after all. Now she's going to wake up on her hundredth birthday with no present. And she's going to think that I've let her down completely," he added miserably.

"Oh, you great goose, she won't think that!" Mrs. Bird said.

"Won't she?" said Paddington. He looked around at everyone's faces. They all seemed strangely excited.

Mr. Brown exchanged a cryptic look with the others. Then he beamed and said, "Come with us."

The family helped Paddington out of bed and led him down the stairs.

"What are all these people doing here?" Paddington asked in surprise.

The hallway was packed! The whole neighborhood had come to wish Paddington well.

Mr. Gruber waved up at him. "Here he is!" he said to the gathered friends. "Paddington's here!"

Everyone turned to look up at him and they burst into spontaneous applause.

Paddington could not believe his eyes as he scanned the crowd. "What are you all doing here?" he asked.

"We wanted to say thank you," said Miss Kitts.

"Thank you?" Paddington repeated, looking puzzled.

"For everything you've done for us," said one Miss Peters.

The crowd murmured and nodded their agreement.

"If it wasn't for you, we'd never have met," said the

Colonel, putting his arm round Miss Kitts.

"You helped me pass my exams," said Fred Barnes.

"And I would be permanently locked out of my house," said Dr. Jafri.

Paddington turned and looked at the Browns. He was feeling rather overwhelmed.

Mr. Brown put a hand on his shoulder. "I'd say you have rather a lot to be proud of, Paddington," he said.

Mr. Gruber chipped in. "When we heard that the police wanted the popping book for evidence we thought we'd get Aunt Lucy another present," he said.

Dr. Jafri nodded. "So we all clubbed together," he said.

"I pulled in a few favors from my old air force chums," said the Colonel.

"And we think she's going to love it," said Mademoiselle Dupont.

Paddington was baffled. "But . . . what is it?" he asked.

"You wanted to get the book so Aunt Lucy could see London, didn't you?" said Mrs. Brown.

Paddington nodded.

"Well, we thought why look at London in a book when she could see the real thing?" Mrs. Brown explained.

As she said this, the doorbell rang.

Paddington looked at Mrs. Brown, not daring to believe.

"Why don't you go and answer it?" Mrs. Brown said, nodding toward the door.

Paddington did as she suggested. His friends stood aside as he walked down the hallway to the door. He opened it, and there, on the doorstep, standing in the snow, a suitcase in her paw was . . .

"Aunt Lucy!" cried Paddington.

"Oh, Paddington!" said Aunt Lucy, pulling him into a warm embrace.

"Happy birthday, Aunt Lucy," said Paddington, and his face lit up with a look of perfect joy.

EPILOGUE

Things worked out well for everyone in the end. While Paddington enjoyed showing Aunt Lucy around London's famous landmarks, his friends Knuckles, Phibs, and Spoon were enjoying themselves too. They had been granted parole for good behavior and were spending their days setting up a lovely tearoom, selling the cakes they had learned to make in Portobello Prison.

Meanwhile Phoenix Buchanan had taken their place! He wasn't letting prison get him down, though. He lost no time in finding a way to put on an extravagant musical number for the other prisoners. He may not have been a success in the West End, but he was doing very well inside.

As he said, "It seems all I needed was a *captive* audience!"